Objective: POTUS

by Stephen J Feins

From Stephen Feins' Bookshelf

- Historical Fiction
    - Stein's Odyssey
    - George Washington, Defendant
    - Two Steps Forward
- Romance
    - The Next Chapter: What the Heart Wants (with Emelie Bonin)
- Fiction
    - The Flow
    - The Eighth Step
    - The Million Dollar Investigation
    - Who Is Jason Foster?
    - The Odyssey of the U-996
    - Brains Enough
- Mystery
    - The Sacred Foot Murders
    - Case of the Twisted Judgement
    - The Case of One Too Many
    - Project Spider
- Crime and Justice
    - The Illusion of Cutter Bay
    - Twelve Honest Women
    - RV Justice: Misfits with Badges
- Science Fiction
    - The Thaxsis Protocol
    - Potten's Folly: Earth
    - Battle of the Dark Star
    - Gamble at Point Zero

Dedication

Law enforcement is under attack from all sides of the political spectrum. These men and women dedicate their lives to protect and to serve. As in many organizations there are those who would profit from, or abuse their position, which raises skeptics and worries in the general public. We must never lose sight of the 99 percent who do a job many of us would never even consider.

The accounts and descriptions in this book are fictional and any resemblance to any person, living or dead, is purely coincidental. Any use of any part of this work is prohibited without the permission of the author unless used in legitimate critique.

Chapter One

"He is going to ruin the country! Why did they ever elect him President?"

Frank 'Bull' Bellows, CEO of the Merger Group, was at his ranting best. He was seated with other CEOs, CFOs, and COOs at their weekly breakfast get together. Heads were nodding as he continued to attack the character and ability of the President.

"Frank, you have been saying these things for two years now. I think it is time for you to change the record."

Frank shot an evil look at Bill Nathan, CEO of LandRush. "We must get rid of this guy before he bankrupts all of us."

Thomas Blander was elected President by the thinnest of margins--only ten electoral votes. The country was badly divided between the upper economic class and the fast-disappearing middle. Unemployment was at seven percent and inflation stood at eight percent. The mood in the nation was barely civil. Now Blander was going to veto a trade bill that would give Frank over ten million dollars and his company would see its stock soar.

"I tell you, this President bends over for any group the press plays up."

Bill leaned forward. "He is the President for the next two years and maybe the next six. Why don't you run for office and show the country how it should be run?"

Frank threw his napkin down and walked out of the dining room of the Estates Men's Club. He headed to his office just down the street and was still mumbling to himself. His company, Merger Group, had seen a loss of thirty-five percent in the stock market and client billings were down almost as much. As a lobbyist, he knew his Board of Directors would not back him much longer.

As he entered his office he found two men waiting for him. One was Gregory Manners, his loyal assistant who asks no questions, and the other was a complete stranger.

Frank walked behind his desk, picked up a pen and threw it across the room. "Greg, are the Hudson reports ready?"

"Yes."

"And who is this person?"

Gregory motioned for the man to come forward. "This is Alan Murphy and he has an idea on how to solve our problem."

Frank looked at Murphy. He was about six two with a large build and looked about forty with salt and pepper hair, thick eyebrows, oval face, and aviator glasses. He was dressed in jeans and a sweatshirt and stood totally erect which meant he probably was ex-military.

"Tell me Mr. Murphy, just what problem are you here to solve?"

Murphy smiled. "My group lends its services to solve difficult problems. Your assistant, Mr. Manners, contacted us and invited me to meet with you. I am referring to the President Blander problem."

"President Blander?"

Frank was caught off guard. He stared at Murphy while he was trying to process the answer he got. Murphy began to walk around the office looking at the paintings and bookshelves. "Greg, just what the hell is going on here?"

Greg was seated beside Frank's desk. "Mr. Murphy is an acquaintance of mine. We served in the army and I saved his life. Ever since, he has been looking out for me. I told him about your concerns with President Blander and how the country was rapidly becoming the laughingstock of the world."

Murphy walked up to the desk. "Members of our group served honorably in defense of this nation.

We are not going to stand by while Blander destroys it."

"Just what did you have in mind?"

"We need to remove Blander from office."

Frank thought this might be a setup. "Are you working for some government agency or police department?"

Greg stood up beside Murphy. "He's an honest guy and I trust him with my life. You can, too."

A number of things ran through Frank's brain. No President Blander means no veto of the trade bill. The trade bill was worth ten million dollars to Frank personally and a hundred million dollars to his clients. His party in the Senate had passed the bill by only one vote meaning they could never manage to override a veto.

Frank pushed on. "Okay Mr. Murphy. How do you get to a man who has more security around him than most nations have in their armies?"

Murphy shook his head. "It's amazing how you can run this big company and not understand politics and the people."

"What do you mean?"

"If we kill the President he will be quickly replaced by the Vice-President who will continue the old policies and veto the trade bill. In addition, Blander will become a martyr and a hero, something we do not want to happen."

"Okay Mr. Murphy. Just what do you propose?"

"We kidnap the President and hold him for twelve days. When he returns to his office the trade bill will have become law without his signature and without any chance of a veto."

Frank looked at Greg and then back at Murphy. "Kidnap?"

Chapter Two

Senator Ralph Sturges was as nervous as an expectant father would be pacing around a hospital waiting room while his wife gave birth. He had worked for eight months making deals and compromises in order to get the trade bill in the Senate. His count told him the bill would pass by one vote. Now he had to worry about President Blander's veto.

His office was 'busier than a beehive' to use an old expression. Members of his staff were working the phone lines trying to keep those who promised to vote for the bill in line. He hoped that more members of Congress would join them in order to override any veto, but he was not successful. If Blander vetoed the bill it would be dead.

An intern stuck his head into Sturges' office. "Sorry Senator but Irwin Reynolds will not change his position. He still is a no vote."

"Okay, keep trying and let me know if anything changes."

Just as the intern was leaving he turned around. "Oh, there is an urgent message from Frank Bellows. He is on line three."

Sturges picked up the phone. "Frank my friend, what can I do for you?"

"I would like to meet with you in your office. I have something to discuss that is best said in person."

Sturges had enough on his mind that he did not want to play games. "Look, Frank, I appreciate all you have done for me but at the moment things are a bit tense."

"What if I told you I have solved the veto problem? There will be no veto."

That was something Sturges would make time for. "I have an hour free at eleven. Can you be here at that time?"

At a little before eleven Frank Bellows, Alan Murphy, and Gregory Manners walked into Sturges' office. "Gentlemen, welcome. Let me call my staff aide and we can get started."

Frank shook his head. "It would be best if just the four of us talk."

"That sounds rather ominous. But okay, what do you have in mind?"

Murphy took the lead. "We plan on kidnapping the President."

Sturges' jaw dropped and his eyes widened to their limits. He said nothing but slowly backed away from the group and sat in his chair. He knew the next thing out of his mouth had better be something cautious. "Kidnap the President? I'm afraid you have come to the wrong person."

Frank pushed Murphy aside and placed both hands on Sturge's desk as he leaned over. "Just hear Murphy out. I was skeptical at first but he does make a lot of sense."

Sturges had to make a quick decision. What they were talking about was treason, a Federal crime that would put him in prison for life with no parole, or face the death penalty. Each second seemed like an hour. It seemed as if he was blinking his eyes in slow motion while his heart was racing.

Frank persisted. "Just hear him out."

"Okay but if I don't like what he says, you and he are out of here and I will deny we ever met."

Murphy moved forward. "Killing the President would make him a hero and his policies would be enacted, including the veto of the trade bill. By kidnapping we force the government into inaction as they cannot replace the President until he is found, dead or alive."

Sturges nodded. "Okay but the vice-president will take over and she will veto the bill."

"She cannot legally take over until there is a determination of the President's ability to rule. Remember, the bill has to be vetoed within ten days or it goes into law. We only need to control the President for that timeframe."

Sturges pushed. "It would seem after five or six days the Cabinet would remove the President for the sake of the country."

"But the President will not totally disappear. We will ferry him to different locations so he can be spotted. We hide him, display him, and hide him again. After the bill passes we can release him as it does not matter what he does then. We just disappear."

Sturges sat back and did not move. It was a wild plan but it just might work. The President would not be harmed, the investigation of what happened would take years, and the trade bill would be law.

Murphy laid out the plan on how the President could be moved to new locations, brought out into the public view, and then hidden. Since they were working with the real President, the kidnappers would make sure his DNA and fingerprints were left behind at every stop. The police would be one step behind and none of the investigating groups would figure out that he was kidnapped.

Frank laughed. "The FBI and the Secret Service will blame terrorists and be chasing bad leads. The NSA and the CIA and other groups will be searching overseas. And all we have to do is be careful when we transport the President."

Sturges raised an important concern. "How will you control the actions of the President when he is out in public? If you use drugs he will appear drugged. And you cannot threaten his family as they will be under a blanket of protection."

Murphy collected his notes. "There are things that motivate people to do what they would never agree to. Trust me, we have the method."

"One last question. What do you get out of this?"

Murphy smiled. "Five million dollars."

Chapter Three

Murphy met with his crew and began planning the kidnapping. He needed to keep the group small and use only those he knew from the army. Each member of the team would get five hundred thousand dollars and a promise that their families would be taken care of it they got caught.

"Gentlemen, and I use that word loosely…."

The three team members laughed and hurled insults at Murphy.

"Okay, enough. You all realize that this operation could go sideways real fast. You each have your assignments. For safety reasons you will not be told the names of your employers or the reason for this action."

Billy, a recent retiree from the army, looked over the plans. "There are a lot of unknowns and no room for surprises."

"If you want out, you're out."

"No way. We will pull this off and I will be sitting on a beach in Aruba next week."

Murphy rolled out a map. "We know President Blander visits his mistress on Wednesday evenings."

Frosty looked up. "What's his wife doing?"

"Exactly the same thing. She is meeting with her 'special guy'."

Peter raised security issues. "Do they have any electronic devices in play? And where is the Secret Service?"

"The Secret Service parks across the street so people in the building won't be curious and investigate which gives the President privacy. Only one agent watches the back."

Billy shook his head. "Why do they stay married?"

"Politics. Anyway, the mistress leaves by ten o'clock to go to her nursing duties at the hospital. That leaves Blander alone for an hour before the security team comes for him."

Frosty spoke up. "What does Blander do for the hour? He should leave right away."

Murphy nodded his head. "It would be a smart thing for him to do but he needs to shower and clean up leaving no clue of his evening activities. He can't afford a lipstick smear or perfume on his body."

Peter raised a concern. "If the Secret Service is out front and in the back, how do we get Blander out of the building?"

"Out the back door. I have a diversion all set to draw away the Secret Service guard."

Murphy laid out the rest of the plan. "The condo is on the top floor and there is a crawl space above it. Frosty will be there with the tranquilizer gun he will take from his job at the zoo. He will loosen the recessed light in the bathroom and let it hang by the wires."

"Won't Blander see it hanging?"

"He will be too busy getting dressed to notice. Now Frosty will shoot Blander from above and refasten the recessed light."

Peter discussed his part. "I will be waiting in the back stair landing and come forward, pick the lock, finish securing the recessed light, and finish dressing Blander. Frosty will join me and we will bring Blander down the back stairs."

Murphy was next. "I will be in the back stairs with a dog. When you come down with Blander I will open the door and throw the dog out. The Secret Service guard will chase after the dog thinking it escaped. We then drag Blander to Billy who will be in the car. That's it."

The room was silent. They were trying to picture all the pieces of the plan and what could possibly go wrong. On the surface the plan looked simple but the execution would depend on timing and if Blander and the Secret Service was where they were supposed to be.

Billy asked the last question. "So we bring Blander to the safe house and wait there. When does all this happen?"

Just then Murphy's phone rang. "Hello?"

It was Frank Bellows. "Murphy, the vote is on Thursday. You need to get Blander this week. Can you do it?"

"No problem, sir."

"Good. You will bring him to the safe house where Greg will take charge. How do you intend to subdue Blander?"

"We will use a tranquilizer gun."

Frank stressed his concern. "Remember, we need him alive."

Murphy hung up and addressed the crew. "Gentlemen, we have a go for this Wednesday night. Everyone must be in their positions by ten o'clock. Billy, make sure you stay out of view from the Secret Service car. You better steal a van so we can lie Blander down."

Frank hung up and was feeling better about the plan. He had his part to do as well. He needed to invite Vice-President Mason out to his ranch for some R & R, the euphemism for offering a large donation from his PAC. This would also give him an alibi.

Chapter Four

Special Agent in Charge David Foster of the Washington, D.C. bureau arrived at precisely eight o'clock on Thursday morning at the Federal Courthouse. He used the stairs to the third floor for exercise. Being six feet and weighing in at one hundred and seventy, Foster fit the ideal measurements for the FBI. Just shy of his thirty-fourth birthday, he was the youngest SAC in the Northeast. If one followed his meal regimen you would never see a fried food or anything loaded with sugar.

"Good Morning, Agent Foster, there is a very strange message for you from Marie Perkins. I wrote it down just as she said it."

Marie Perkins was the Deputy Chief of the Secret Service and as such she was assigned to the President's protection detail. Foster and Perkins shared a comfortable relationship that never quite got into a more romantic one.

Foster looked at the message which read 'Missing 911'. He picked up the phone. "Marie, its David, what the hell is going on?"

"Are you on a secured line?"

"Yes."

Marie took a deep breath. "POTUS has disappeared. We cannot locate him."

Foster thought he had heard wrong. "You mean he is out of touch?"

"No. He is nowhere to be found. We have searched every inch of his last location and found nothing. I need you and your department to help us."

"I will meet you at Francis' Coffee Shoppe in thirty minutes."

Marie was already at a back table holding a cup of coffee. Foster made his way over stopping for a cup of tea. "Well, Marie, give me the full story."

"President Blander was at his special friend's apartment with our people outside watching the front and back. He was supposed to come down at eleven o'clock but he never showed. Our people went to the apartment, went in, and there was no sign of Blander or a struggle."

"Anything out of place? Any blood?"

"The apartment only had Blander's and the nurse's fingerprints and DNA. The only thing out of place was a recessed light in the bathroom ceiling. There are no cameras and we had to be very careful interviewing the neighbors. No one heard or saw anything unusual."

"Damn! When this hits the fan a lot of heads will roll. Do you think he was taken or he just walked away?"

Marie looked around to be sure she was not overheard. "We don't know. We haven't told anyone yet, not even his wife, and we have a total media blackout."

Foster shook his head. "What would you have me do?"

"I need you to do a full background search of Blander because if we do it people will be curious and suspicious. If he walked away there must be something in his past that he is running to or from."

"Is there anything else you can think of?"

Marie looked off into the distance and suddenly snapped her head back to face Foster. "Yes, I don't know what it means, but one of the tenants thought their dog was stolen but it was found by one of our agents."

Foster finished his tea, pushed back his chair, and stood up. Unfortunately there was someone behind him and he collided with her. "I'm sorry. I did not see you."

The slightly bruised woman smiled and laughed. "I'm okay. No damage. I hope you have insurance to cover this."

Foster heard what she said but could not for the life of him understand what she was saying. "Yes, I am glad you are okay. I will be more careful in the future."

Just then Marie stood up and started to walk away. "Call me."

It was one of those moments when everything came together and created a brewing storm. The woman was Susan Star, a reporter for the Washington World. The whole scene finally hit her. "You're David Foster and she is Marie Perkins. I'm a reporter for the Washington World. What's a top FBI agent doing meeting with the Deputy Director of the Secret Service in an-out-of-the way coffee shop?"

Foster panicked but he did not show it. He had to cover the meeting but sometimes the coverup could lead to more trouble. "Please, this is rather a private meeting and I would ask you not to write about it for personal reasons."

Star saw a story and pushed. "Personal reasons? What does that mean?"

"Miss Perkins and I are very close friends and we were discussing personal matters away from the office and prying eyes."

"That sounds like a romantic meeting."

Foster was in too deep and was about to get in even deeper. "Yes, you could say that. But our careers might be impacted by our being together. I would ask for your discretion."

Foster handed her his card with his cell phone number on it. He promised her an exclusive if anything further happened. She put the card in her pocketbook and watched as he left the shop. So, two single people have a romantic get-together. It was nice and no reason to pry. Or was there?

Chapter Five

President Thomas Blander struggled to wake up. He was dizzy and had a throbbing headache. He looked around and did not recognize his surroundings and knew he was not in his girlfriend's apartment. He hoped to see one or two of his secret service detail but the room was empty.

Slowly he rose up from the bed. He tried shaking off the groggy effects of some kind of drug. He was not bound and the room even had a window with no bars. Perhaps he was in an accident and some kind person took him in not realizing who he was. He got up and started to walk, which was more of a wobble.

"Mr. President, I am glad you are feeling better. You must be hungry and in need of something to drink. I am sure you have questions and I will do my best to answer them. But first, let's eat."

Blander followed the man who was wearing a face mask, not exactly the way a good Samaritan would look. There was a galley area and a long table with two other individuals eating. He looked at the clock and it was a little after eight, in the morning. He had slept all night.

"Who are you and what do you want? There will be no ransom and if you call my detail I will put in a good word with the police."

The men all laughed. "Mr. President, we have no intention of releasing you for the next twelve days. And you can be sure, if you go along with our requests, no harm will come to you."

"I demand to know who you are and why you are holding me!"

"Easy, Mr. President, calm down and have some breakfast."

Blander sat at the table and one of the men put a plate of food in front of him. There were scrambled eggs, toast, home fries, and sausage links. "Why won't you tell me what you want?'

"We want you to think of this as a vacation and in a little more than a week you will be back at work. We are keeping ourselves covered for our protection, and quite frankly, for yours as well."

A cell phone sounded and the man by the stove answered it. "Ya, we're good. Any word on how to proceed. Okay, we'll do that. No, he has not been hurt and has no idea where he is. That's what we were thinking." The man hung up.

"Okay, our boss just told me the bill has passed and the clock on the ten days starts now."

Blander dropped his fork. "What bill? Ten days means it will become law without my signature."

"Very good, Mr. President. So you see there is an end to this whole thing."

Blander played along in order to get more information. "How about you tell me which bill?"

"I guess it won't hurt. It's the free-market bill that lowers tariffs and cuts the tax on goods by fifteen percent. In addition, it cuts the sanctions on Chinese trade."

Blander became agitated. "That's the special interest bill that hands corporations a huge tax break. It also cancels the new high earner's tax rate for those making two hundred thousand dollars or more, and eliminates the estate tax."

"Well, Mr. President, you are up on everything now. You promised to veto the bill and we could not let that happen."

"How many votes did it pass by?"

"One. So you see if you vetoed the bill there aren't enough votes to override."

Blander started to play with his food. "This is all about greed and control by the corporations. My Vice-President will veto the bill the same as I would."

"I'm afraid you have not quite got it. Yes, if you are unable to perform your duties the Vice-President steps in. But since no one knows where you are, or if you are at some high-level secret meeting overseas, you still are the only one who can execute policy and sign bills."

"And by holding me it means there are not enough votes to override my veto."

"Now you are catching on. So, enjoy the next few days and if you do what you are told…"

"I will be released. But how are you going to keep this quiet and yet convince people that I am alive and well?"

"That's the genius of the operation. We will take you to different locations each day so you can be seen. That will be reported and stop any attempt to replace you."

"Supposing I won't do it? If you kill me you can't keep the fiction alive that I am still capable of running the country."

"We do not intend to kill you. But you will go into some stores or restaurants to be seen and then return to this house."

"How can you be sure of that. I could just as easily ask for help and the clock stops on the bill.

The twenty-fifth amendment will kick in and then it won't matter if I am your prisoner."

One of the other men at the table stood up and walked behind Blander. "You think we haven't planned for that? Your immediate family is well protected but your lady friend is not, nor is the general public."

"What have you done!?"

"We have your lady friend in another room and she will pay a high price for your refusal. We have also planted explosives in high traffic areas which will kill many and wound hundreds more. You won't be hurt but a lot of other people will. And all you have to do is let a bill become law."

Blander was having trouble taking it all in. Was the bill so critical that it was worth the lives of his lover and hundreds of civilians? Besides, once back in power he could push a repeal of the law by Congress. And when word got out of what happened to him, the nation would rally around him and he would get the votes to overturn the new bill.

Meanwhile Greg had set up the first public appearance for that afternoon. He also wrote the script for what Blander would say at each viewing. The plan was coming together nicely.

Chapter Six

The Vice-President arrived at Bellows Ranch. "Madam Vice-President, welcome to my humble ranch. I hope your trip was pleasant."

"Frank, it is always a pleasure to get away from the confusion and noise that is our nation's capital. But please, I am off duty so call me Alice."

Frank Bellows had a crush on Alice when they were in college together. She was always out campaigning and pushing causes; he was taking business courses on how to make money. They dated and were almost engaged but they found out they were more friends than romantic partners. Frank was still an old bachelor and Alice was married with two children.

Frank led her to the back porch where they could take in the vast view of the open range. Over the years Frank had used his lobbyist money and connections to stopping three different housing plans and one shopping center, to protect his land. Alice was a frequent visitor to the ranch and seemed to enjoy it more and more now that she was Vice-President.

Frank had a pitcher of lemonade all set on the porch. "May I pour you a glass?"

"Frank, you spoil me. But don't stop."

"So where is your husband today?"

Alice sat down and played with the moisture on her glass that sat on the table. "Jon is on another quest to save some other endangered species. He packed his bag and was gone before I even woke up today. I love him but he is not very supportive. What I need is a husband to run my office, one who will watch my back."

Frank took a sip. "Your chief of staff, Paul, must be out there pushing your agenda."

"Paul has decided that he knows too little about D.C. politics and while he was on target when I ran for governor, on the national scene he just isn't up to it."

"I'm sorry to hear that."

Alice sat up straight and leaned over the table. "Okay, let me get right to it. Paul is out and I would like you to be my new chief of staff. You know the players and you know the politics. I know we would make a magnificent team."

Frank was surprised by the offer. Yes, he had wanted to be one of the power brokers in D.C. but he had no 'in'. With the job of chief of staff he would be in the White House and in touch with all the power people. Still, he was hesitant to take the job because her husband knew about their previous romantic relationship.

"I'm very flattered, but there are two stumbling blocks."

"If you are worried about Jon, don't be. He has lost interest in our marriage but we stay together for the kids and my political career."

"I'm sorry about that but my economic goals are not in sync with yours. Take the new trade bill. Blander will veto it and if anything happened to him you would veto it."

Alice sat quietly, slowly sipping her drink. "Blander and I were on the same page, but the economy is rapidly collapsing and those who contribute to our campaign may not do so when re-election comes up. Perhaps I will run against Blander. I know you were behind the trade bill and I think I could live with that."

Frank could not believe his ears. With her on board, the trade bill would never be challenged and his role in his company would be solid. If he took the position he would also be closer to Alice and perhaps get the chance he never got in college.

"Alice, I am very interested but there are a number of things that I have to handle. Besides, how will we work together with the past we shared? I don't know what your feelings are, buy mine have not changed."

Alice was caught off-guard. She knew Frank was still in love with her but she did not know if she was in love with him. They would need time to sort things out. Frank also was in the middle of the kidnapping plan.

A Secret Service agent came up on the porch with his cell phone. "Madam Vice-President, there is a coded red call for you from the White House."

"Frank, you will have to excuse me. I have to take this call."

Alice walked down off the porch and listened intently. Frank could tell by her facial expressions she was being told very bad news and that had to be that the President was missing. Alice came up on the porch. "Frank, I have to go. Let's keep our discussion on hold. We still must deal with Blander in some way."

Alice got into an SUV and three cars sped out of the driveway. Frank was confused as to his options but this could mean a bigger break than he imagined. If Alice replaced Blander he would be the chief of staff for the President of the United States. Only Blander stood in his way. He walked into the house and called Greg.

Greg answered the phone and went into another room away from the President. "Frank, is everything okay?"

Frank paced around the room and finally sat down on the couch. "Greg, I am thinking about changing the plan."

"It's a little bit late but I will see what I can do. What exactly are you thinking about?

"Blander will eventually talk and we don't know just how much he knows."

Greg thought Frank was panicking. "All the men are wearing masks and they have never used a name or nickname. I am pretty sure we are in the clear."

"I just had a conversation with the Vice-President who told me she supports our trade bill and would not veto it. Therefore, we no longer need the elaborate plan we have put together."

Greg was confused and beginning to worry. "So, what are you saying?"

Frank took a deep breath. "We no longer need Blander or have to worry about eliminating him. I would be in a position to protect all of you."

Greg's mouth dropped. "You mean kill the President?"

"Is that something you and your men could do?"

Greg was either in shock or denial over what he heard. Could he kill the President of the United States?

Chapter Seven

Special Agent David Foster always looked forward to visiting with Senator George Sloan, his favorite 'uncle' (not his blood uncle). He had grown up with George's son, Barry, from the second grade until college. He was best man at Barry's wedding and the Godfather to little Maryann.

"Senator Sloan, it was nice to get your invitation to spend the afternoon with you. I spoke with Barry last night and I hear there may be another little bundle coming your way."

Sloan was in his third term after serving as Governor and Member of the House. He knew everyone who was anyone in D.C. He had nominated David for West Point. He considered David a nephew.

"David, this is not a social visit. I wonder how much you trust me. Would you share information that was confidential or being kept secret? I'm not talking about classified material."

David was not sure what was on George's mind. "I trust you with my life and with my career. If it is at all possible I will fill you in on just about everything. But what is this all about?"

George leaned back in his chair and put a lollypop in his mouth. He had started the habit when he quit smoking ten years ago. "I know a lot of people in government and in the press. One of my media friends called me this morning and asked me about any romance that was brewing between the Deputy Chief of the Secret Service, Marie Perkins, and Special Agent in Charge David Foster of the FBI."

David could not help smiling. "Let me assure you there is no romantic thing happening between Miss Perkins and myself."

"I thought so. But it made me curious to know why there was a secret meeting between you and Miss Perkins. It's way out of character for both agencies."

David was perplexed and not sure of how to proceed. "You know how grateful I am for everything you have done for me. Barry is like a brother. I will let you know what is going on but you must promise what I tell you will never be revealed."

Sloan pressed his desk phone command center. "Terry, no calls and do not interrupt even if the office is on fire."

David began the short version. "Last night President Blander was visiting his lover. When she left he took a shower and got dressed but he never came downstairs to go back to the residence. When the agents finally entered the apartment there was no sign of him. No one has been able to find the President since."

Sloan bit on the lollypop as he clenched his teeth. "Damn. Has the President been kidnapped or has he walked away?"

"That is what Marie and I were discussing. We have merged our resources and have imposed a blackout on the media. Then just before I got here Marie sent me the strangest message. Blander showed up at the 'turn the dirt' ceremony at a construction site. He joined other bigwigs, turned over dirt, then jumped into an SUV and took off. He never said a word."

Sloan needed time to process. Putting the facts together it raised more questions than it answered. "We have to rule out kidnapping and go more with he is running away from something."

"Or he is running to something, or rather someone. He may be planning on disappearing with his lover.

"You mean his mistress. No, he has worked much too hard to throw it all away. He remains the President until we know exactly what is going on."

David's phone rang and he looked at the screen. "It's someone named Susan Star. Do you know her?"

"Yes, that's my source in the press. She is the one who called me yesterday."

"How did she get my private number?"

"I'm afraid that is my fault. I did not want to raise any suspicion about your meeting and she only wanted to confirm the romance."

David nodded his head. "If I answer I have to lie, which is par for the course in D.C.. I think it best to ignore her."

Sloan shook his head. "I find when a good reporter is ignored they begin to think there is a coverup. She will dig into the story. You had better answer."

David pressed talk. "Hello, this is Special Agent in Charge David Foster. How may I help you?"

Susan Star was a very good reporter. She turned on her recording device. "Agent Foster, thank you for taking my call. I talked with Senator Sloan and he gave me your number. I hope you will not be angry with him."

David laughed. "No, I will not be angry with him, I just won't fix anymore of his parking tickets."

There was dead silence. David panicked. "I am only kidding. I can't really fix his tickets because the FBI doesn't do parking tickets. What I mean is even if I could, I wouldn't. Hey, help me out here."

Susan was laughing so hard she had trouble speaking. "Don't worry, that will not appear in tomorrow's newspaper. I just called because a romantic relationship between two top law enforcement individuals is news."

"Well, let me ease your mind. Miss Perkins and I are not romantically involved. At all. In any way. In any sense."

Susan decided to push it. "How can I believe you when you were at a secluded back table at a dimly lit rendezvous table."

David's voice got louder. He was beginning to feel as if he had dug himself into a hole. "Look, Miss Star, I am still dating other women and as far as I know Marie is dating other men."

"How can I be sure of that?"

Foster was trapped. "Why don't we have dinner tonight? Say seven thirty at the White Column?"

"That's very exclusive. I heard there is a waiting list of weeks."

"Please, meet me at seven thirty and I know you will enjoy the evening."

David had stumbled his way into a dinner with the press. Susan on the other hand smiled as she hung up. Dinner with a high-powered justice department source. Men are so easily confused.

Chapter Eight

"Well, Mr. President, you did a great job. You kept your word, did the groundbreaking, and never tried to escape."

Blander's face was red. "It wasn't easy! Now you keep your part of the deal and leave my friend and the general public safe."

The four men watching the President had all used makeup to hide their faces. By adding putty to broaden their faces, false moustaches and beards, and dark glasses, no facial recognition program would identify them. Blander never saw the uncovered faces.

Billy locked Blander in his room. "What gives? I have never seen you so upset. You're drumming your fingers on the table and have a frown on your face. Give."

Greg was not in the mood to be pleasant. He figured the time had come to divulge Frank's new orders. He was not sure how the others would take it. "You and the others have a seat. Things have taken a turn."

The rest of the crew came in with very worried looks. Have they been identified? Are the police on their way? "Look, Greg, whatever it is we can work it out."

Greg swallowed loudly. "Frank has an idea that he and the Vice-President have hit it off. She wants to make him her chief of staff and he believes she will be his mistress or next wife."

Billy smiled. "All right, the old guy is gonna get it on!"

Frosty slapped Billy on the arm. "Shut up Billy. Greg, go on."

"Greg says that the Vice-President agrees with his position and we no longer need to keep the President as a prisoner."

Frosty put it all together. "No, damn it, no! We are not killers! I am not going to participate in killing Blander!

Peter and Billy said nothing. They looked at Greg with vacant stares. They had not signed up for this and even if they decided to go ahead with it, the authorities would hunt them down for the rest of their lives. They would always be looking over their shoulders and no amount of money was going to turn them into killers.

Billy was the first to catch his breath. "Look, Greg, we will follow you anywhere at any time. But this is way out of anything that we are comfortable with. Is a trade bill that important it can take a life?"

Greg's head was bowed and his arms were crossed across his chest. "You guys are not seeing the whole picture. Frank thinks he will become the next First Gentleman after the Vice-President becomes President when Blander's body is found."

Frosty added another wrinkle. "What makes Frank think he will be the next First Gentleman? She may be leading him on to kill Blander and then turn on him. She may be setting him, and us, up."

Peter finally weighed in. "I know you owe loyalty to Frank, but perhaps he is asking too much of you. Would you kill Billy or Frosty if Frank said to do so? And if Frank really wants to clean up this whole thing, what makes you think he is going to let us live? And that includes you."

Now Greg had a lot more to think about than just killing the President. All the scenarios his men had laid out could very easily happen. If Frank was ready to kill for his ambitions what would stop him from betraying him and his men?"

Blander picked the lock and walked into the room. "I see the great think tank is coming up with my next performance. How about I go to a supermarket and give a short talk on how I plan on bringing the prices down? Maybe a hospital visit with wounded veterans?"

"Shut up Blander!"

The President wasn't used to being told to shut up. It gave him a clue that things were coming apart, but just how bad it was he did not know. Maybe this was the time he should try make friends with one of his captors and get some information from him. There were only seven more days before the time runs out for him to veto the bill.

The crew dispersed and headed off to get ready for the next showing. Greg still had his head down and had not moved. Blander figured this was the best time to drag out information. "So, you're the leader of this band of misfits. The thing I can't figure out is why this bill is so important to someone. Help me out here."

Greg looked up. "The trade bill will lower the tariffs on certain goods which will cause other nations to lower their tariffs on our goods. The second part of the bill lowers the tax rate on corporation profits from fourteen percent to six percent."

"So it is a matter of money, no surprise there."

"Our employer's company represents the products that you placed in tariff to force other countries to lower their tariffs. But no other country has reduced their tariffs."

Blander was beginning to understand. "And the pay of CEO is based on profit and stock prices which have dropped rapidly. Many CEOs face replacement."

Greg stood up. "That gives you the full picture about the kidnapping to keep you from vetoing the trade bill. Unfortunately things have taken a turn for the worst. The plan has gotten ugly. I have to go now."

Blander returned to his room. He now had an idea who was behind all this. He was remembering the shouting match he had at a conference with CEOs when he first threatened to veto their trade bill. The loudest, and most obnoxious taunts came from Frank Bellows who came very close to threatening Blander.

He now had a way to get out from under. If he made it known he had figured it out, he could put pressure on the captors to give up with a promise of immunity. But wait, it might also make him expendable, so he had to proceed carefully.

Chapter Nine

Susan Star was still enjoying her latest coup as she entered the restaurant to meet David Foster. She had him so confused that he agreed to meet with her and answer questions. She was wearing a very revealing dress that exposed enough cleavage to entice, but not enough to look slutty. David was a good-looking man and under different circumstances she might just make a move or two but this was business.

She stopped by the hostess. "Hi, I'm supposed to meet Mr. Foster."

"Yes. He is seated in the patio section. Please follow me."

The patio was decorated with flowers and strings of lights overhead and on poles designed to look like trees. The tables were intimate size and had flowers wrapped around chair and table legs. David stood up as she approached and walked to meet her. This seemed well beyond a business dinner. He was dressed in a very flattering suit and tie, his hair trimmed neat, his face clean shaven.

"Miss Star, you look lovely this evening. I'm so glad we have a chance to get to know each other."

Susan was caught off guard and did not know what to make of all this. Surely he was not expecting a date or some kind of romantic meeting. Maybe this was all an attempt to throw her off her game. "Do you hold all your business meetings at this restaurant?"

Foster smiled. "Only those with very beautiful women."

"Okay, okay. I get it. You are being sarcastic and trying to mess with my head. You have no romantic feelings toward Marie Perkins."

Just then a woman came charging into the restaurant and headed for the patio. "What the hell are you doing here? I had to chase you through three phone calls to find you."

Foster dropped his head to his chest. Susan spun around and it took a minute to focus on the woman. "Deputy Chief Marie Perkins I presume?"

"Yes. And who might you be?"

"I'm Susan Star of the Washington World about to have a nice dinner with Special Agent Foster. Do you object to that?"

Perkins quickly pulled a chair from another table, sat down and slammed a folder on the table. "Believe me, Miss Star, it is Miss, I assume, David can have dinner with anyone he wishes."

Susan laughed and was about to leave when she saw one of the photos which had slid out of Marie's folder. It was a picture of the President at the turning the dirt ceremony, but the circles on the photo were around the Secret Service detail charged with protecting the President. "Yes, I was there today. Very nice picture of President Blander."

Foster needed to make some sense out of everything. "Miss Star, please forgive Miss Perkins…"

"Deputy Chief Perkins."

"Yes, Deputy Chief Perkins who has no boundaries when it comes to work and relaxation. Some call that having a life. The Deputy Chief and I have been working on a difficult case and it appears she needs my input right now. May I have a rain check?"

The woman who had left the vacant chair was back and standing directly behind Perkins. "Excuse me, I believe that is my chair you are sitting in."

Susan stood and started walking away. "It's okay, she can have my chair. I thought Foster had an interest in getting to know me but he lacks proper manners."

"I'm really sorry. Please, a rain check? I promise it will go better next time."

Susan was out of earshot by then having stomped her way out of the restaurant. Foster could not tell if she was really mad or if she was playing some game with him.

"Marie, what the hell are you doing here?"

"I'm sorry, David, but I had to talk with you. And by the way she is a very good-looking lady. You seem to have caught a big one, perhaps an eight or nine?"

"Stop that! It's complicated, but you can be sure I have no interest in Susan."

Marie smiled. "Susan is it? Wow."

Foster threw his napkin on the table and loosened his tie. "Alright, what is it?"

Marie took out all the photos. There were circles around the heads of the Secret Service team who were protecting the President. "Take your time. Look carefully at the scene and tell me what's wrong with these pictures."

Foster studied the photos. Perkins handed him a magnifying glass. He bent over until he was on top of the photos. "Okay, here is what I see. First, the team are still standing around the car and not taking up positions around the President. Second, they have a lot of facial hair which is against protocol. And last, the car is a plain SUV and not an armored number."

Marie took back the magnifying glass. "Bingo! The President was escorted by phony Secret Service men which raises more questions. When the press tried to ask questions the President rushed to the car. Now that is not unusual but this was a perfect time to blast Congress for the trade bill and announce his veto."

"Okay, just what are you saying?"

"The President is a prisoner of these men and the threat is so deep that Blander is unable to escape."

Foster had to admit this was a bad sign. "You think the President was kidnapped and is being held for some ransom or something. But if that's the case, why bring him out in the open? It does not make sense."

"And that's why I need you now. Something major is about to happen and I want to get in front of it."

"As do I."

Chapter Ten

Susan Story, a dedicated reporter without any social life, sat at her desk trying to piece together some very strange happenings. Since when does a President show up for a photo opportunity and not say anything to the press? Why did his protection detail stand by the SUV and not in the crowd? And why only three agents?

As she sat back she began to think about the possible romance between Perkins and Foster. He was a good-looking guy and was fun to mess with. Had the dinner not been interrupted who knows what would have happened. She shook her head as if to erase her thoughts. Still, it would have been nice to see where it went.

"Star, get your butt in here!"

It was the call of the editor. When it came to social behavior and protocol he never got the message. One day she would sue him for a hostile workplace and retire on the millions of dollars she would get.

Star walked into the editor's office. "Star, what happened to that romance?"

"No story there."

"I want you working on this tip I got. Frank Bellows, big CEO and lobbyist, has had a private meeting with Alice Mason, the VP."

Star looked at the message. "I'm sure it was just another attempt to bribe her for something."

"That's what I thought until she called in her staff and reversed her decision on the trade bill. She just undercut her own President and abandoned her position of two years. Maybe it was more than an attempted bribe."

"You think she was bought off? But what difference does it make, Blander will veto the bill this week."

"That's the problem. Blander hasn't been seen or heard from over the last three days. Then he pops up at a minor dirt turnover ceremony and won't even talk to the press. My source in the White House says something is very wrong. Deputy Chief Perkins is running wild and scared. Do you know her?"

Star nodded. "Yes, we just met. I think I might have a source that will fill in the blanks."

"Okay, take the story. I need it for tomorrow's final edition. Now get that sweet butt out of here. I have real work to do."

Star went back to her desk. This gave her an excuse to call Foster and set up that 'rain check' dinner. She picked up the phone.

"Hello, Special Agent David Foster, how may I help you?"

"Agent Foster, this is Susan Star, the date you deserted last night."

Foster was not happy. "Yes, Miss Star, I am so happy to hear from you. What can I do for you?"

"You can feed me for one. You owe me a dinner at that fancy restaurant and I'm collecting on it."

Foster thought for a moment. He needed to meet with Perkins to go over film taken from reporters who were at the dirt turnover. "I'm afraid it is far too late to get reservations, Miss Star, perhaps at a later date."

Star could not let Foster slip away. "A gentleman would honor his commitments and in this case I would settle on lunch."

Foster could slip away for lunch and get the date over with. "That sounds very doable. How about we meet at the Blue Onion at, say, one o'clock?"

"I look forward to it."

Foster called Perkins to make his excuse. "Marie, I can work this morning but I have a lunch date with someone."

"Probably with that tramp I saw you with last night."

Foster was taken by surprise. "Wait a minute. She's no tramp. What has gotten into you? You've never been like this."

"I'm sorry, David, it's just that I am worried and afraid there is more going on than we know."

"Look, I told you I would help. I just need about an hour at lunch to finish off a promise I made."

"She is rather attractive but she is with the press. Be very careful about your pillow talk."

Foster was getting upset. "What the hell do you mean by pillow talk? I will keep our meetings a secret."

"I see the way she looks at you. It's the way I used to look at you."

"What are you talking about? You told me long ago that we had no future together. You sound, if you pardon my French, a little jealous."

"Perhaps I was too hasty and too full of myself when we were together. It has been almost thirteen years.'

"Yes, thirteen years."

Perkins suddenly went silent and he could hear her breathing in the phone. Suddenly she was back. "Sorry, I apologize."

"No need for that. Should I still meet you at your office?"

"Yes, please. We need to get to work and have no time to waste."

It seemed like a contest as to who would hang up first. After a short time Perkins did. David sat there with the phone in his hand unable to figure out just what was happening. And what about Susan Star? Was she looking for more than just a story?

Chapter Eleven

Blander was back in his room filled with 'what if's. The plan to just kidnap him and then let him go seemed to be slowly fading away. For the first time he was able to see the faces of two of the four men and he could hear them arguing like never before. When someone says 'I can't do it' when talking about a kidnapped person, you begin to fill in the blanks with very negative ideas.

Greg was no closer to deciding than any of the others. He was the leader, not the boss of a criminal crew. His men trusted him and would take a bullet for him but killing a President was a stretch too far. "I'm going to talk with our employer. You make sure Blander gets to the next gig and does not mess up."

Frosty nodded. "We'll get it done, boss, we'll get it done."

Blander backed away from listening at the door. He was about to be taken to a second location to be paraded around. It was day four of the kidnapping and time was running out. He considered writing a help message and trying to hand if off to someone. Perhaps he could simply turn and run and let the public know something was not right. No, it had to be subtle because his lady friend and the general public were at risk.

So how do you come up with a plan? Blander turned on the television, went to the streaming services, and started to watch every television program or movie where a person held captive managed to escape. Of course he wanted to watch the whole show as the last part was about revenge and the cruel and bloody way the bad guys' lives were ended. And then he saw it, the perfect plan. But did he have time to get it ready? He would have to pull it off.

The kidnappers entered the room bringing his suit and tie. "Put these on. We need to be out of here in about an hour. Don't try anything or your loved one will pay a steep price."

The hour went by slowly and Blander tried to get up his courage. It was strange that the script he would follow came from a show where police used a tactic to plant a message using the media. He closed his eyes and tried to picture what he needed to do. He was placed in the SUV and off they went.

"Okay, Mr. President, this is a simple visit to a VA hospital. You will shake hands with some wounded veterans, have a picture taken with the doctor and a patient, and then it's back to the SUV."

Blander nodded. "I will be calm and at least I still am doing some good while I'm your prisoner."

"Yea, sure, just so long as you don't try anything like making believe you are ill and collapsing on the floor. I have an injection here that will pick you right up."

Blander smiled. "Do you think I would really try that old dodge?"

They entered the hospital and walked to the second floor where there were newly wounded veterans. Blander walked around, shook hands with the injured, and smiled for photos. The press started to throw questions at him but he raised his hand. "Please, no questions. These brave men have given their all to protect our country and they deserve respect."

Frosty shook his head. "Damn…how can we kill him?"

The hospital photographer came in to set up a picture. Blander leaned over one of the beds and bumped into a tray table spilling food on his shirt. "Sorry, I got some kind of a stain."

Frosty was not sure how to handle it. He needed the pictures to be taken for the internet so millions would see the President was alive and well. Blander turned to the attending doctor. "I have an idea. I can put on a doctor's coat and cover up the stain."

Frosty thought for a moment. "Yea, that could work. Get him a coat."

The attending physician went into a closet and returned with a coat. Blander took off his jacket and slid the coat on. The photographer cleared away the onlookers, including the phony Secret Service group, and began to focus his camera. Suddenly Blander made a break for it running down the hall and into a stairwell. Frosty and his men ran after him.

Billy reached the front door and did not see Blander. Frosty and Peter searched every room on the floor. Members of the press started asking questions of Frosty who had just returned to the hospital room. "The President got an emergency message through his head set and has rushed back to the capital. Thank you all for coming."

Frosty knew that would not track very well but his most important task right now was to find him. He could not understand why the President ran because of the threats he was under. Suddenly Blander came walking calmly down the corridor with his hands by his side. "Were you looking for me? I needed to use the rest room in the most urgent way. I hope I didn't worry you."

Frosty called the others and they gathered by the SUV. "That was very stupid. If you did anything to warn the authorities it will mean your loved one will pay a very high price. Now get into the car."

Greg was not happy to hear about the incident. He called Frank. "I don't know what he did but it seems he did not contact anyone as we have heard nothing. The press from the hospital did not mention it. I think we can continue with the original plan."

"I don't care! He is getting bolder and bolder with his attempts. Now it's time to get rid of him. I'll get back to you after I check with someone."

Frank picked up his second cell phone and pressed an automatic dial button. "Hello, how are you? One quick question, what if the President's body is finally found? Are you still on board with not vetoing the trade bill and the position as your chief of staff?"

Alice Mason took just seconds to reply. "As I told you earlier I find you very competent to handle my 'affairs'. I will put you in contact with my new press secretary, Alan Murphy."

"Thank you, Madam Vice-President"

Chapter Twelve

Foster walked into the office of Marie Perkins and found people searching the internet as if looking for buried treasure. "Good morning, Agent Perkins, I can see things are quite busy here."

Perkins looked up from her desk. "David, things are getting really weird and I need your help."

"That's what I'm here for. What do you need."

"I have a Mr. Kusserman in my outer office. He wants to sue the Secret Service for damages done to one of his apartments, the apartment Blander disappeared from."

Foster laughed. "You have got to be kidding."

Marie got up and David followed. "Mr. Dusserman…"

"That's Kusserman."

"Sorry. This is Special Agent Foster of the FBI. He handles all damage claims for the government."

David was caught by surprise. "Ah, yes. That is why I am here. Tell me Mr. Kusserman, what was the extent of the damage?"

"Well, I have broken bureaus, chips in the wall, torn up rug, and damage to the sink in the kitchen. I will need to totally renovate the kitchen."

"I see. That is a lot of damage. If you give me a moment I will look at the video."

Kusserman started to breathe heavily. "Video? What video?"

David stopped and sat down. "When government agents search a place they always take video in case they miss a clue or we damage the place being searched."

David stood up again and started to walk out of Perkin's office. "Hold on there, Agent Foster, perhaps I am thinking of the wrong apartment."

David sat down again. "It's the apartment of Laura Watts, a nurse."

"Oh, that apartment. The only damage there was to a recessed light in the bathroom. It was a little loose and when I pushed up on it something stuck me."

Marie and David looked at each other and then at Kusserman. "What exactly stuck you?"

"This funny looking dart. Here, I have no use for it."

David grabbed the dart. It was brand new and the writing on it indicated it was part of a set used at zoos. "Mr. Kusserman, I could kiss you. I will have that light fixed immediately. Let me know when Nurse Watts is there."

"Sorry, I do not know where Nurse Watts is. She left to go to work three days ago and I got a call looking for her. She hasn't been seen since."

Marie and David jumped up and hurried out of the outer room. Back in her office David grabbed the phone and called the FBI lab. "Blacke, Foster here, send someone over to the Secret Service headquarters and pick up evidence. And I mean now!"

"I'll send Tom. While I have you on the phone something weird has happened."

"Look, Blacke, I don't have time. You handle it."

"David, give me a minute."

"Go. You have sixty seconds."

"The local D.C. police contacted us about an Amber Alert they got."

"Blacke, I am losing patience."

"The alert came from the hospital's call-in emergency system this morning and the missing person's name is Thomas Blander."

David froze. Blander was at the hospital at the time of the alert. Could that have been a message from the President. "Blacke, what else was on the alert?"

"Instead of a license plate it was an address with the letters SOS after it."

David looked at Marie. "Damn, that guy is clever. I think we now have Blander's location."

He returned to the phone. "Blacke, ready SWAT team Apple and meet me here. I want it on blackout terms, no discussion about the target."

David hung up. "Well, Agent Perkins, are you ready to be reunited with your President?"

The two left the office and ran to the parking lot. Just as they were getting in to their car, one of the agents ran up. "Chief Perkins, the tranquil dart came from Midtown Zoo."

David started the car and sped out onto the street almost striking another car. Horns were blearing as he drove and swerved down the street. "It all fits, Marie, someone removed the recess light and fired a tranquilizer dart at Blander. Then they entered the apartment and took him out."

Marie suddenly shouted. "Yes!! It's the last piece of the puzzle."

"What are you talking about?"

"I was just about to fire one of my agents. He was supposed to be guarding the back door of the building but he left his post to go after a kid's dog. That ruse would have given someone time to take Blander out of the building."

SWAT was already at the location in a secluded area about a block away from the address David gave them. "Jack, this is Special Agent Perkins of the Secret Service. We know President Blander is in that house. Have your men surround the building but keep out of sight. Get some eyes inside."

The SWAT team moved quietly. Using scopes they looked inside the rooms and there was no movement of any kind. Using heat scopes there were no images either. David gave the order to move in and they slowly took up entry positions. After a minute a signal was given and the men rushed in. There was shouting and sounds of things breaking.

The commander of the SWAT team came walking out of the house. David and Marie ran up to meet him. "What did you find? Is the President okay?"

"They are all dead."

Marie shrieked. "Not the President! No!!"

The SWAT commander took off his helmet. "There was no sign of the President. Just four guys who have been murdered. We'll get forensics over here and identify the bodies."

Marie turned and buried her head in David's chest.

Chapter Thirteen

Most law enforcement agencies were either using zoom online or at the FBI headquarters for a meeting run by David's boss, the Secretary of Homeland Security. The room was crowded with twenty people including Marie's boss who was sitting beside her. It was time to fill in all the other agencies and put together a task force to hunt down the people responsible for the kidnapping. The room was noisy but David's boss drew everyone's attention.

"Special Agent Foster will run down the information we have to date. I would ask you hold your questions until after the briefing. Agent Foster."

Despite his years in the Bureau, speaking to this kind of group made him very nervous. They say public speaking is the most nerve-racking thing a person can do. "Ladies and gentlemen, here is what we know. A plot to kidnap the President was initiated by a group who wanted to keep the President from vetoing the new trade bill. The kidnapping took place at the apartment of Laura Watts who has since disappeared."

"Do you believe she was part of the plan?"

"Not at this time."

"What about those bodies found at that apartment?"

David was losing patience. What is there about holding all questions these people did not understand. "The kidnapping took place on the day the trade bill was passed. For three days the President was paraded around so he appeared to be still in command. On the fourth day he was able to send a coded message by way of an Amber Alert. A SWAT team entered the apartment and found four people dead and the President still missing."

"Have the four men been identified?'

Foster took a deep breath. "Yes. They are all ex-army. The apparent leader, Greg Manners, was the personal assistant of Frank Bellows. The other three, John 'Frosty' Frost, Peter Gains, and William 'Billy' Todd were part of a team working for 'Solutions', a private security firm run by Alan Murphy, who is also missing."

"It seems you have a lot of missing people. Has Frank Bellows been questioned?"

David did not want to answer as he knew the reaction. "No. It seems Frank Bellows is missing."

The room broke into many subconversations and the noise level rose. It was so loud that people seated next to each other had trouble hearing. Finally Foster had had enough. He took off his shoe and banged it on a table. "Shut Up!!"

That brought the room to silence but also brought reproach to Foster. Just then the door opened and a man came in, handed Foster a note, and left. Foster shook his head. "I have just been given new information. At nine o'clock this morning Frank Bellows was found murdered."

"Any idea who killed Bellows?"

David was happy to move on from his outburst. "We have put every agent on the hunt for Alan Murphy."

Foster's superior ended the meeting and made arrangements to share any and all new information. Marie walked over to David and put her hand on his shoulder. "They really threw you under the bus."

"That's why I get the big bucks!"

The two slipped out of the room and down to David's office. "I don't think Bellows was the mastermind. I have my people looking at Bellow's and Murphy's financials. They say you can solve a lot of crimes by following the money."

An agent opened the door. "Excuse me, there is an urgent call for Agent Perkins."

She took the call. "This is Deputy Chief Perkins. I am putting you on speaker."

"Chief, Ryan here. Senator Sturges just called and wants to see you immediately. It's about the President's location."

Marie hung up and bolted out of the office with David one step behind. Was Senator Sturges part of this whole thing? How did he know where Blander was? How many others were involved in all this?

They arrived at Sturges' house and found it surrounded by D.C. police. "I'm Deputy Chief Perkins. What's going on?"

"I'm Captain Falls. We were called by the Security System alarm that there was a break in here. When we entered we found a person who looks like President Blander hiding in the basement. Senator Sturges was lying dead on the parlor floor."

Marie rushed past the police barricade and into the house. There was President Blander seated at the kitchen table drinking juice. "Marie, so very nice to see you. And you are…"

"David Foster, Special Agent of the FBI."

"Well, agents, it is very nice to see you both. Now let's get me back to the White House and clean up this mess. It seems very strange that this is all about the trade bill."

"How did you get to Sturges' house?"

"It was very weird. The leader of the kidnap group suddenly let me go and I fled to my old friend Sturges' house. He took me in and called you people."

Marie led the President to her car. "What happened to Senator Sturges?"

"A strange man was about to shoot me when Sturges came to my rescue. They fought a bit and then I heard a gun go off. Sturges fell to the floor. And at that time I could hear sirens so the stranger pointed the gun at me but it just clicked. I suspect the gun jammed or he ran out of bullets. Anyway, the guy fled."

"I'm glad you're okay. Your use of the hospital's Amber Alert system really helped us find you."

"Yes, that was quite a gamble. Now get me to the White House as I have a bill to veto."

On the way to the White House, Blander called his staff and his wife. Marie was driving with David in the seat beside her. She was humming and smiling. "We did it. We rescued the President. Case closed."

David shook his head. "Sorry Marie, but this whole thing doesn't add up. There was a lot of money and people involved in a very complicated plot just to stop Blander from vetoing a bill. And now we have six bodies."

"What you're saying is we have missed something big."

"Yes, Marie, I'm afraid we have missed something very big.

Chapter Fourteen

Foster had ducked calls from Susan Star but now that the circumstances had changed there was no reason to avoid her. The press had played up the kidnapping and of course put out at least five theories as to who did what to whom and why. He called and offered to honor his 'rain check' and they met at her favorite diner for lunch.

"Hello Miss Star. I'm sorry it took so long for us to reconnect. I hope you are hungry as I am sure I owe you the biggest lunch you want."

Susan was dressed in a skort which emphasized her long, smooth legs. Her top was form fitting with a bare midriff. Her blond hair sat neatly on her shoulders and she wore just enough makeup to make it appear as if she wore no makeup at all. She had a wide smile for someone with such a tiny mouth. She was definitely not going to work dressed like that.

"Special Agent Foster, it may have taken a long time but we are here together at last. May I call you David? You can call me Susan."

"You look exceptionally nice. I hope I am not delaying you from some headline grabbing news."

Susan laughed. "You, my dear David, are my groundbreaking headline news."

Foster was not sure what she meant but he played along. "And just how am I groundbreaking news?"

"You were the primary investigator on the President's kidnapping along with that woman…"

"Deputy Chief Marie Perkins."

"Yes, yes, her. But I have a feeling there is more to the story than what my fellow reporters wrote about."

"I'm sorry to disappoint but it's all out there."

Susan picked up her menu. "Okay, we will play your game. But first I am famished and I am on a lunch hour deadline. I recommend the Caesar Salad with chicken."

"I'm sorry Susan but men do not eat vegetables. I'll just settle for the mountain cheeseburger with fries."

Susan laughed. "Given your body I would never believe you ate anything like that, ever. You must weigh in at about one eighty, right?"

"My weight is a government classified secret."

"Well, the government really put you together quite well. I wonder what they could do for me?"

"From what I can see you need no help. Mother nature has taken excellent care of you."

"Why Mr. Foster, I do believe that was a compliment. You do have a human side after all."

The server came over and they ordered lunch. They made small talk about their families, where they grew up, and what schools they attended. Neither had alcohol and Susan's foot kept bumping into David's leg. They finished by talking about the case.

"Tell me David, if you were dating someone, would it all be classified and kept top secret? Are you allowed to be seen with a woman? Or a man?"

"First of all, it would be a woman. And secondly I was seen with you, however briefly, in public."

"I remember. We almost had a moment until that lady broke in."

"Agent Perkins had critical information about the kidnapping of the President. I would consider that ample reason to break in."

"How long have you and Agent Perkins been dating?"

"That's a rather personal question. We did date in college but that was almost thirteen years ago."

"Are you taking part in the dating scene or do you swipe left or right?"

David tried to look innocent. "I'm not into social experiments."

"Come now, a professional person like you who is busy every day. I would think dating apps were designed for you."

David picked up his coffee. "I do not need to use an app. I meet individuals and if I think there is an interest I ask the person out."

Susan smiled. "Okay, you just had lunch with me. Do I fit the interest level that would cause you to ask me out?"

David began to see where this was going. What was he afraid of? She was a very beautiful woman and very smart as well. She could give as good as she could take. More importantly she was not in law enforcement which would add different perspectives to conversations. "Let me say, if this were a normal meeting, I would definitely ask you out for dinner and the theater."

Susan brushed her hair back and put it into a ponytail. She shook her head and leaned forward. "I would probably accept."

"What do you mean 'probably'? I don't think I'm ugly or boring."

"You are neither of those so I'm going to take a chance and accept your invitation to a play and dinner. Perhaps we could get tickets to 'Mister Richard's Lover' which is on stage at the Crescent Theater. There is a nice restaurant right around the corner from there."

David was getting in deeper and deeper but he did not seem to mind. "It is impossible to get tickets for that play."

"You remember how we got into that fancy restaurant due to your connections? Well, you leave the tickets to me and I will call you with all the details for Friday night."

"Yes, Friday night it is."

Susan got up, as did he, and she smiled. "Don't worry, I do have a long dress."

And then she walked away. David watched her every move.

Chapter Fifteen

Marie Perkins headed for the office of Special Agent in Charge David Foster for a special briefing. She thought about her relationship with him when they were in private school. They had great chemistry and they would argue about world events until early in the morning. There was no doubt that she was in love with him and he with her. But graduation brought the stumbling block of career direction.

It was 2009 and they were seated in the Chapel awaiting the start of the graduation ceremony. There still were questions about whether there would be a religious opening but the graduates really did not care. They just wanted their diplomas and to party all night, or all week. Marie and David were alone on the pew talking about the future.

"Marie I have to leave for West Point in four days. Senator Sloan, my unofficial uncle, got me the slot. I think we should get engaged before I leave. I know it's short notice but we can have a wedding after my first year."

"David, my love, you will be facing new challenges and you don't need a fiancée to tie you down. Besides, I will be in California at the police academy. Having a coast-to-coast relationship would be difficult at best.”

“I’m just afraid we will lose each other.”

“Darling, we will never lose each other. We have to be patient and I know everything will work out. Now let’s make these last four days a time to remember.”

And that was it. Over the next four years their letters and phone calls became fewer and fewer. David was off to Afghanistan with his Military Police unit and Marie graduated at the top of her class at the California State Police Academy. They dated others but each time it ended in breakups. The reunion came when David was assigned to D.C. with the FBI and Marie was promoted to Deputy Chief of the Secret Service and also assigned to D.C.

It was 2020 and David was attending a friend’s wedding. “David, my best man, I want you to meet my Sara’s maid of honor, Marie Perkins.”

They looked at each other and did not know what to do next. Should they shake hands? Should they hug? Should they just nod? “Marie, you look as beautiful as ever. You haven’t changed a bit.”

“You two know each other? Great! I’m sure Sara will be thrilled.”

They finally got to talk with each other at the reception. Marie had not said much and had kept her distance throughout the ceremony. Her first task was to support the bride and David and the groomsmen were just a little hung over from the bachelor party.

"Marie, I meant to write but you moved so much I could not find you. How have you been? Is there a special man in your life?"

"David, I admit I have missed you and I still have very strong feelings for you. I love you but I might not be in love with you."

David nodded. "It has been fifteen years."

"You always did that. Back in high school if you told a story about your childhood it was fifteen years ago. Why are you so in love with 'fifteen years'?"

"It's just an expression, kind of like when you get sick or hurt it takes four to six weeks to heal."

Marie smiled. "Well, it has been thirteen years but perhaps we can see each other to catch up, maybe once a month."

David knew it was a lost cause. He could not figure out this 'love and in love' stuff. After the wedding they did occasionally see each other at parties and for work but Marie kept her distance. It wasn't until recently when Susan Star entered the picture that Marie became, it seemed, jealous. But now they were part of a kidnapping and attempted murder of the President of the United States.

Marie entered the meeting room and noted it was filled with men. There was only one other woman there, typical she thought. The men on the other hand were very pleased as she was tall, slender, and her business attire showed curves in the right places. Her brunette hair was short and surrounded her face like a picture frame. Her eyes were light brown and her nose was of the button type. When she smiled her whole face seemed to glow.

"Marie, come and sit by me. We have a special guest who needs no introduction."

Just then the door opened and President Blander entered the room. Everyone stood up and Blander started to shake hands with all the attendees. He wanted a full briefing and he was going to answer questions about what he had observed. The meeting was run by the Secretary of Homeland Security but even he deferred to Blander.

"Welcome Mr. President and ladies and gentlemen. We…"

Just then almost every cell phone started to ring. There was a bit of panic as everyone tried to shut them off while looking at the message coming in. Finally the Secretary looked at David. "What does 'package available' mean?"

David looked up at the Secretary. "Alan Murphy has been captured. He is in Interrogation Room Four. If you turn on that monitor I will send the feed from Room Four and all of you will see the interrogation live."

"Get going!"

As David rushed out the door Marie stood up and ran after him. "David, take me with you!"

Marie came up behind David who reached out his arm and took her outreached hand. They took the stairs not wanting to wait for the elevator. They arrived at Room Four and found David's assistant standing outside.

"Where did they find Murphy? Did he put up a fight? Is everyone okay?"

"David, you will not believe this. We didn't catch him. He called, surrendered, and walked in with his attorney. He wants to answer all questions and charges."

David looked at Marie. "This is going to be very interesting."

Chapter Sixteen

Alan Murphy was dressed in a blue suit and red tie with shoes that cost more than the national budget of a small country. He was accompanied by his lawyer, John Sigmond from Sigmond, Sigmond, and Frair. On the other side of the table sat David Foster, Marie Perkins, and Sally Reynolds, recorder. Murphy would only talk with Foster and Perkins but had agreed to allow the session to be broadcast to the upstairs meeting room.

David took the lead. "Mr. Murphy, thank you for coming in. We have a number of questions concerning your activities over the past four days."

"Agent, I want it recorded that I am here of my own free will and I can leave at any time unless there is an arrest warrant presented."

David began. "Would you please state your name and occupation?"

"Alan Francis Murphy, former Army Ranger and now CEO of 'Solutions', a private security firm."

"Did you know Greg Manners, staff assistant to Frank Bellows?"

"Yes, we were in the service together. He recently approached my firm to provide protective services for his boss, Frank Bellows. I assigned three of my personnel to the protection detail."

"There is no record of Frank Bellows asking for, or in need of, protection. Were you aware your men were involved in the kidnapping of President Blander?"

"I have no knowledge of that. I took Manners at his word that he wanted protection for his boss."

Foster figured all of Murphy's answers would be of the 'I did not know" variety. "And were you aware that Greg Manners was in charge of the kidnapping crew?"

"Totally unaware. I'm sorry he was killed but I had nothing to do with his actions."

Marie was getting tired of the slow pace. "We have traced a payment by Bellows to your account for two million dollars. That seems rather extraordinary when the industry average for protective services is five-hundred thousand."

"Agent Perkins, when you want the best it costs."

Marie pressed. "Well Mr. Murphy, it seems your detail was not up to the task. Who could have surprised your elite group? Someone they knew and trusted, perhaps?"

"I was in Germany setting up a branch of my agency. You can check my passport."

Foster pushed. "Why should we believe you? You don't seem very upset by the deaths of your personnel and your good friend Greg Manners."

Murphy laughed. "The two of you are typical government dupes. You are so concerned with the little happenings that you miss the big picture."

Foster leaned forward. "Why don't you paint the big picture for us."

Murphy looked directly into the camera that was mounted on the wall. "The kidnapping was only a diversion. The real reason was to assassinate President Blander."

Foster and Perkins both pushed their chairs back and stood up. "What the hell are you talking about?"

"As I said, the kidnapping was a diversion. It was designed to keep you wasting your time and resources into solving how the trade bill fit in to the kidnapping. The kidnappers would kill Blander and make it look like an accident. It was someone way high up who was running the plan."

"And just who is that?"

"All I know is whoever gave the order to kill the President is still out there and will try again. He or she has already proven they can get to the President and disappear leaving no trace."

Sigmond closed his briefcase. "We are done here. Alan, let's go."

"Alan Murphy, you are under arrest."

"And what are the charges?"

"Withholding evidence of a credible plot to kill the President."

Sigmond stood up and turned to leave. "Mr. Murphy answered all your questions and has no further knowledge of any action that might be taken against the President. Send the warrant to me."

Foster and Perkins were livid, their faces almost a bright red. David made a fist so tight that his fingernails cut into his palms. Perkins rushed in front of Murphy to keep him from leaving. But it was all for nothing as there were no facts on which to hold him.

Upstairs, the mood in the meeting room was raw. Everyone was voicing their own theory of what they should do and how they should do it. Blander was the only one who sat silently as if he might know something. Foster and Perkins entered the room.

The Secretary of Homeland Security began yelling at the pair. "Well, you made a mess of that! I have never seen such a poor display! Just what do you think we can do now!"

Foster was equal to the tongue lashing. "We got everything we could. We now know that this whole trade bill fiasco was a cover for a larger plot. Being aware means we can protect the President and continue to investigate."

Perkins followed up. "David is right. I will draw up plans to further protect the President."

The Secretary was breathing rapidly, face contorted, and he was waving his arms as if trying to swat a swarm of bees. "You! Are you serious? The two of you are off the case. Turn in your badges! Now get out of here!"

Foster and Perkins looked at each other and decided to walk away. As they reached the door an FBI agent caught up with them. He handed them a note from the President. They were being summoned to the Oval Office.

Chapter Seventeen

Being summoned to the Oval Office was both a thrill and a worry. Marie had been in the President's Office on several occasions but it was a first for David. They arrived at the same time and were seated just outside the office. Marie sat tall and had a smile while David fidgeted and frowned every so often.

"The President will see you now."

And with that short sentence the duo stood in front of the most powerful person on the planet. "Please, sit down and make yourselves comfortable."

They walked over to a couch and sat. An aide asked if they wanted something to drink but they both declined. The President then cleared the room except for Marie and David.

Blander took out a file. "I have read every report filed on the kidnapping case and I find the two of you work well together. Given Mr. Murphy's cryptic message I think you would agree this situation is far from over."

Marie was more comfortable with the President. "Yes, Mr. President, Agent Foster and I both agree things do not add up. Unfortunately we have been removed from the case, and in fact from our positions, by the Secretary of Homeland Security."

Blander sat back. "Well, the Secretary works for me and many times he's an idiot. He means well but he believes only his men can solve crimes. As of now, you are both reinstated and are assigned directly to me, and only me. You will have no other cases or duties. Understood?"

David finally spoke. "Yes, Mr. President."

"Now that that is cleared up, I have something to tell you that must be kept classified. If you find the information hard to accept, let me know and you will be relieved of your duty. I am trusting you to be honest and discrete."

Marie and David put down their recording devices and notebooks. "Whatever you tell us will remain in this room and be shared with no one else."

Blander leaned forward, sweat appeared on his forehead. "I have been seeing a woman on Wednesday nights for some time now. You probably think that my wife was in on the plot to kill me. But what you do not know is we have an open marriage. I have a lover as does my wife. There is no jealousy or hard feelings. I am telling you this because I want to shelter my wife and my lover from interrogation.

If the press gets ahold of it there would be a feeding frenzy."

Neither Marie nor David made a move. "Mr. President, we are aware of your open marriage and figured that your wife and your lover had nothing to do with the plot to kill you. You can rest assured that we will not be interrogating either lady."

Blander smiled. "I knew you were the best. Since my poll numbers are low and I was caught in a bind over the trade bill, members of my own party wanted me to veto the bill while members of the other party wanted me to stand down. That is why I believed the kidnapping was about the trade bill. Now we know differently."

Marie picked up on it. "So the kidnapping ended just in time for you to veto the bill and pleased your party. Since you were held hostage the other political party could not attack you. Because you bravely went ahead with the veto it pleased the general public over the bravery you showed. So you came out of this on top."

The President laughed. "I was afraid I was going to be a suspect in the deaths of those four kidnappers along with Frank Bellows."

David took out a cell phone log. "You made calls from the hospital on their land line. One call went to the 911 line and was the Amber Alert. But a second call went to Senator Sturges' private line."

"Yes, when I overheard the kidnappers talking about killing me I knew I had to do something to escape. I knew we were going to a hospital where if I wore a doctor's jacket I could get into the doctor's lounge and use the phone."

David finished the story. "That's when you issued the Amber Alert and called Sturges to come and help you."

"Yes. Had I realized Sturges would be killed I would never have involved him."

Marie added the obvious. "It all comes back to Murphy and what he knows but he isn't talking. We need to find him and turn him into our witness."

David began writing things down. "That brings us to Laura Watts, the woman you have been seeing."

Blander replied. "She has no connection. I am worried that she has disappeared. I want you to find her."

Marie stood up and started to pace. "The person who gains the most is the Vice-President. She has been seeing Frank Bellows and could have used him to take over the kidnapping plot and turn it into an assassination attempt."

"That would be hard for me to believe but if you think there might be something there then go for it."

Blander stood and extended his hand. "I trust you both. Thank you for not judging me. Remember to report only to me at any time day or night. Here are two appointment letters and passes to enter the White House at any time."

Marie and David left the Oval Office and felt as if they had just walked out of a sauna session. "Let's go to my place and put this all together."

David smiled. "That means some great home cooking. As I remember it you almost became a chef."

"And that's all your getting, good food."

"What, no dessert?"

Chapter Eighteen

Marie's condo was on the top floor of a ten-unit building. David wanted to take the elevator but Marie insisted they take the stairs for some good cardio exercise. They walked into a very sparse looking living room. Television, computer workstation, couch, one reclining chair and a couple of floor lamps. Off to the left was the kitchen area with all its gleaming stainless-steel appliances. And to the right was a bedroom and bathroom.

"Wow, this place rivals the Taj Mahal. How do you afford such grandeur on a government salary?"

Marie threw her briefcase on her desk. "Look, this place is located just a block away from the office and I can walk to shopping, restaurants, and clubs."

"Where do guests stay?"

Marie glared at him with very wide-open eyes. "The guests stay at their own homes!"

"From what I can see that bed is at least a queen or maybe even a king. A lot of room for one person."

Marie walked over to David, put her arms around him, and whispered in his ear. "There's enough room for me and anyone I invite."

"Miss Marie, you are making me blush."

Marie sat on the couch and hugged a pillow. "What happened to us? How did we allow careers to pull us apart? I miss you and I think about you often."

David was caught off guard. "What are you saying? I have felt that way for many years. Perhaps it is time for us to take a good look at where we are."

"And would that look include Miss Susan Star?"

David was unsure of what he wanted to say. "Perhaps we should look at the list of suspects before dinner?"

Marie got up off the couch and put her arms around David. She slowly brought her face close to his. She stared into his eyes without blinking and gently, softly kissed him. He slowly raised his arms to embrace her. She backed away and picked up her briefcase. "Let's sit at the table."

David took off his suitcoat and joined her at the table. They spread out all the different pieces of paper and lists. For the first half hour they said nothing as her kiss had taken over his mind. Perhaps this was the moment to act on his instinct.

"David, with most of the participants dead and Murphy unwilling to cooperate we have no leads to follow. Were you surprised when Blander confessed to the open marriage?"

David took a deep breath. "Yes. It seemed a reason for his wife to kill him but after what he said she is out of the picture. Right now we only have two leads, Alan Murphy and Alice Mason, the Vice-President. Murphy I can believe was involved but not the Vice-President."

Marie could not help from laughing. "And look at these twisted romantic triangles. I can't get over Blander admitting to an open marriage and being proud of it. If the public knew, his poll numbers would be at almost zero."

David nodded. "I agree but the divorce will wait until after he is out of office so the First Lady doesn't lose her influence and power."

Marie agreed. "Ah, yes, political power and social prestige. So how are we going to solve this mess and get Murphy to talk?"

David moved over on the couch and started to rub her back. They sat together until Marie fell asleep and his arm began to tingle. He picked her up and carried her to the bedroom. He gently took off her shoes and covered her with a blanket. He then left the room.

Back at the table, David ran through all the information and the known facts. But as he tried to concentrate thoughts of Susan began to occupy his mind. And then thoughts of Marie. He was torn between two women and he knew he would have to make a choice.

David bit his tongue. He ran into the bedroom and shook Marie until she woke up. "David, let me sleep. I was having a great dream, or thought it was a dream."

David sat on the edge of the bed. "We need to dig deeper into Frank Bellows, who was a partner of Vice-President Alice Mason's. She is the one who benefits most from any assassination of the President."

"But how do we prove it? Bellows and his assistant, Greg, are both dead. We have searched their homes and found nothing."

David smiled. "But what about the cloud?"

Marie began to see a path. "But the security of the cloud is such that no one can break in. They have passwords and codes and security questions that we could never break. How would we get the information?"

"What one mind can create on the computer another mind can break."

Marie looked puzzled. "Do you know a hacker who can break into the account?"

"Remember when Murphy said he was in Germany at the time of the kidnapping and murders? This document shows he was in Germany for four days but his hotel records show he was there for only two days. Where was he the other two days?"

Marie picked up the phone. "Roger, I want you to get the complete background on Alan Murphy's trip to Germany. It seems he slipped away for two days. I want to know where he went."

David was on his phone. "Tracer, it's David. I need you to do a job for me hacking into the cloud. Yes, I know you are on probation but I will make it okay. Remember, I kept you out of prison so you wouldn't lose custody of your kids. Okay. I will be in touch."

Marie looked at David. "You have a hacker on your contact's list?"

"Doesn't everyone?"

Chapter Nineteen

It seemed like there would never be another day when Foster could lie in bed until nine, have a leisurely breakfast, and go to the office where there would be no phone messages or a crisis of some kind. He shut off the alarm, grabbed a shave and shower, and headed out to his favorite food cart for coffee and a donut. Just as he was about to order, his phone rang. It was Marie.

"Good morning, Marie. You are up early."

"Good morning to you too. I have the overnight reports and I think all the pieces are beginning to fit into place. I just brewed a pot and my assistant stopped by the bakery for some fattening-looking pastries."

David took off at a quick pace, his stomach making all sorts of noise. He entered the Secret Service building and double climbed the steps to the second floor. There she was, sitting pretty, looking just delicious. The box of pastries was on the desk with its cover open.

"Did you come to see me or my goodies?"

David let out a laugh. "You really don't want me to answer that, do you?"

Marie chuckled. "Grab something and let's head over to the conference room. I have a big surprise for you."

They entered the room where three other agents were working. She led him over to the large computer station. "Okay, Sue, show Foster what we found out about our friend Alan Murphy."

Sue ran the program. "As you can see Murphy is leaving his hotel in Germany and getting into a car. Cameras follow him to the border and he enters France and heads north. He is then out of camera range, but the French police sent a map of the area. It leads into a section near the German border where suspected terrorists have made camp."

David shook his head. "What is Murphy doing in that part of France? Who is he meeting with?"

Marie turned. "Thanks Sue. The puzzle gets crazier and crazier."

One of the agents walked over to Marie. "We have a video call for Agent Foster."

"Put it up on the display."

"David, it's Frank. We were studying the interview you had with Alan Murphy and something strange hit us. He had no reason to look into the camera and mention the threat against the President.

It was almost as if he personally was making the threat. We dusted the room and Murphy never left a print, there was no DNA, and when we checked the records we have, he appears to be non-existent."

David and Marie looked at the video. "Frank, did you run facial recognition?"

"Yes, and that is another thing. Murphy's face and prints should be in the data base because he has firearms at his firm 'Solutions'. But nothing appeared."

David started to walk around the room. He was humming. He suddenly stopped and ran back to the computer station. "Frank, send the video to the French police."

Marie looked puzzled. "French police? Why? He was working in Germany."

"Frank, just do it!"

Marie and David walked over to a corner of the room. Marie sat opposite David. "Let's sit and enjoy some kind of breakfast while we still can."

"Agreed. It will take time for the answer to come back."

They sat quietly occasionally looking at each other. Marie broke the silence. "We need to clear up the famous 'elephant in the room' issue."

"And what would that be?"

Marie put down her food. "I thought about what you said about us and you were right. We put everything into our careers and nothing into our personal lives. I was awake all night running over our days together. And it is obvious that yes, I am still in love with you. Also I am jealous of your relationship with Susan Star."

David wiped his mouth. "I can honestly say I have waited years to hear you say that. But can we live on memories and forget about the time we have been apart? I have always been truthful with you and I have to tell you Susan Star has a hold on me. I don't know how that will play out because it could be just a hormone thing."

Marie laughed. "A hormone thing? What are you, twelve?"

"Aren't you the one who said men never grow up? We are motivated by the lower parts of our bodies?"

Marie moved closer. "I am talking about a long-term commitment, not a one-night stand. Susan is beautiful but if you say it is a hormone thing then I know I have a chance to be with you."

"And I want to be with you. Let's…"

Sue yelled across the room. "Agent Foster, there is an incoming message for you. Only audio."

Marie and David got up and headed over to Tom's station. "I'll play it for you."

"Agent Foster, I am Jean Blanchet, Chief of Police. When the picture you sent arrived it caused all kinds of activity. We know this Alan Murphy very well except not as Alan Murphy. His real name is Ahmad Akbari and one of my men has seen him meeting with the head of the suspected ISIS offshoot run by Behzad Hakimi. I hope my English is understandable."

David smiled. "Your English is better than mine. Please send me all the data you have on Ahmad Akbari."

"Yes, please keep us informed. Hakimi's group is noted for assassinations and terror bombings."

Marie nodded. "I am familiar with Hakimi and the ISIS group."

David turned to Marie. "We need to meet with President Blander. This Murphy imposter was making a personal threat. I am willing to bet the whole kidnapping scheme was devised by him. My guess is he brought it to Bellows."

They were just about to leave when another phone call for David came in. "This is David Foster."

"You are not very formal today. Where is the 'Special Agent in Charge' title?"

"Susan, this is not a good time. Things are moving very quickly and I have to go."

"Fine. Fine. I have some information from one of my sources, a paparazzi who follows Vice-President Mason and her family. I looked at some of his photos and in two of the pictures there appears to be a man who looks like that Alan Murphy you are after."

"DAMN!! I will be right over. I need to see those photos."

"Okay, I'll wait here. Are you coming alone or are you bringing a friend?"

David's head was spinning. Here we had an important piece of an assassination plot and she was worried about my relationship with Marie. "I will be alone. Thank you for this."

David looked at Marie. "Susan thinks she has photos of Mason and Murphy meeting. I am going over to get them."

"And I'm not invited, am I?"

"Look, this is just part of the case. You can put together a presentation for the President and I will meet you at the Oval Office."

David had developed a bad headache and he left the room with his heart racing and his mind full of questions.

"Good morning, I would like to speak with the person in charge."

Alan Murphy was wearing paint-splattered clothes and a painters hat. He was surrounded by four other men in the same gear carrying ladders and paint buckets. While he waited, Murphy looked at a blueprint of the area he and the others would be working in.

"Hello, I'm Lieutenant Mavis, what can I do for you?"

Murphy pulled out a sheet of paper. "We are here to finish up with the renovation that was recently done to the bridge. I have the contract page for the cleaning and painting of the old control rooms."

The lieutenant looked over the contract. "This is very strange. The renovation of the bridge was completed in 2020. I have never heard about more work that has to be done."

Murphy motioned his men to start walking towards the old bridge control room. "You remember the Covid panic? The contractor had to finish the steel and concrete work but the cleaning and painting was set aside. Now that the panic has subsided we were contacted to finish the job.”

“I don’t know. I thought the entire budget was already exhausted. Why would they want to clean and paint these old areas?”

Murphy pulled out another paper. “As you can see, they plan on having tours go through the bridge and the control rooms with all its machinery. They spent over two-hundred twenty million to renovate so they want to get some money back. Besides, the Arlington Memorial Bridge is an important part of D.C. history.”

“Those rooms are very small. Are they sure about letting people go down there?”

“Yep. There is a lot to see. And we will be carving out a room where tourists can sit and have a beverage while they rest.”

The lieutenant laughed. “The National Park Service has really stretched the limit on this idea. What company are you from?”

“Solutions.”

“Solutions? I’ve never heard of it. Well I see all the paperwork appears to be in order. Who signed off on the contract?”

“We are under the direction of the Office of the Vice-President.”

"Yes. I see her signature. Well, take your time and if you need anything let me know."

The lieutenant and the Park Ranger left the area. Murphy turned to his men. "Okay, get the rest of the stuff into the control room. Be very careful not to drop anything or let them see inside the paint cans."

"Where do you want the triggers to be placed?"

Murphy studied the blueprints again. "If we pack it all in sections eight and nine it should control the blast straight up to the roadway. Attach the sensors in section nine. We've got time so let's get this right."

His crew began unloading the rental truck with phony advertising on the side. There were fifty, five-gallon paint cans, along with wires and other electronics.

Murphy pulled out his phone. "We're in. We should be all set by tomorrow. Any news from France? This better go right. Yes, I know. I will be in touch after we finish."

Suddenly the lieutenant came back. "I just got off the phone with the prime contractor and he doesn't remember your company or the order to renovate the old control room."

"We showed you the paperwork. Perhaps the person at the prime contractor is new and wasn't aware of our sub-contract work."

As the lieutenant reached for the land line Murphy spun around and fired two shots causing him to fall backward and onto the floor. "You two, take the body and stuff it into one of the sections."

Murphy went outside and took out his satellite phone. He entered a secure number and was connected to northern France. "It's me. What is going on? Have you done it yet?"

He smiled as he hung up. The plan was coming together rather well. Looking out over the bridge he could picture the destruction and panic when the explosion happened. Anyone on the bridge would be killed and he had a recorded message from Behzad Hakimi taking credit for the bombing.

All Murphy had to worry about was the absence of the lieutenant. He had to come up with some story before the police came searching. He called the private number of Vice-President Mason.

"Alan, I hope you are not cancelling tonight? I have missed you today."

"Alice, I ran into a problem at the bridge. Would you call the D.C. police and tell them you asked Lieutenant Mavis to be part of your security team and he has agreed."

"Okay."

"Thank you my love. And I finally got the good news from France. I will see you tonight."

Murphy sat in the truck and took out a thermos. He had done his job and when the time came the President of the United States would be dead and the Vice-President would be installed as President. He would then be a key player in the White House.

Chapter Twenty-One

David Foster arrived at Susan Star's apartment with both joy and fear. He was not sure if he was happy to be with her or not. He felt more like a teenage boy trying to date two girls and getting away with it. He knocked on Susan's door and took a deep breath.

The door opened and there was Susan wearing a terrycloth bathrobe and a towel wrapped around her head. "David, please come in. I hope you don't mind my appearance but I have a date tonight and I was just getting ready."

David smiled as the top of the robe was very loose fitting and the bottom was short, just above the knees. He sat on one side of the couch while she sat on the other side. "I would like to see those pictures. I have a meeting and those photos are a critical part of the puzzle we are working on. You could have just texted them."

"Yes, but then I wouldn't have you sitting on my couch. I will get them and in the meantime why not pour yourself a drink and loosen your collar. I hope the pictures have what you need and it is not a false alarm."

Susan got off the couch and David watched intently. The sash on the robe was loosening and the robe was beginning to open. He knew the proper thing to do was to say something, or at least look away. Nevertheless he kept watching as she walked toward a desk. She picked up the photos and when she spun around one side of the robe flew open.

"Oh, I'm sorry. This robe has always been a problem. I hope I did not scandalize you or embarrass you."

David took a deep breath. "No problem. I just need to see the photos in order to keep abreast…I mean up to date…with my case."

Susan laughed. "You mean you did not like what you saw? I'm not ashamed of how I look, are you?"

David did not know how to answer. She was a very beautiful woman and just a glimpse of one side of her body was enough to stir him. But this was not why he was here. Susan meanwhile shook her head and took off the head towel with her hair looking as wild and untamed as she appeared to be.

"Tell me David, would you like to stay and have a drink?"

"No. No. I have a meeting I have to get to. And besides, you have a date you are getting ready for."

Susan approached him and squatted in front of him causing the robe to slip open once again. "To be truthful, you are the date I am waiting for. I don't know how you feel about the woman making the first move but I hope it is something you would like."

"Susan, please, I really have to go to that meeting. I would be lying if I said I did not want to stay and spend the afternoon with you but the timing is just not right."

"So you would like to spend more time with me?"

"Oh, God. I would like to devour you!"

Susan got up and closed the robe. "I will be leaving on a two-day trip and I'll be back on Friday. That should give you enough time to decide if you would really like to devour me."

David had trouble getting off the couch due to the reaction of his lower body. He limped over to the desk and sat in a chair. He spread out the photos and picked up the magnifying glass Susan had there. He carefully looked at every inch of the pictures. Without doubt there was Alan Murphy standing next to Vice-President Alice Mason. They both had drinks in their hands and looked happy.

"Susan I can't thank you enough for these photos."

"Why are they so important? I know that Alan Murphy is under investigation but I am sure he has visited with a number of people in the capital before the kidnapping incident. Is he a part of that?"

David started to head to the door. "I'm not at liberty to say more. When this is all over I think you will understand why I could not tell you anything."

Susan walked to the bedroom, stopped, and looked back. "Tell me, how do I compare with your Marie Perkins? She appears to be a bit too tightly wound for you. With your job you need a partner who can help you relax and enjoy life."

"I told you before, Marie Perkins is a friend and we are not dating or involved."

"I'm afraid the expression on your face doesn't support that claim. I will see you Friday night."

David left the apartment and stopped halfway down the stairs. He sat down, took out a tissue, and wiped his forehead. His knees were still a bit weak and part of his brain seemed to be yelling at him for leaving the apartment. He had the pictures and needed to get to the White House as soon as possible. He wasn't sure what condition he would be in.

He entered the parking lot when there was a loud noise and something flew past his head. He felt a stinging on his face and when he reached up he felt liquid. He looked at his hand and it was blood. He immediately dropped to the ground and pulled out his service weapon.

Hearing nothing he slowly crawled over to his car and used it for cover. He began to stand up looking in all directions. Another loud noise and the car windows exploded and showered him with glass. The next sound was a car with spinning wheels speeding off into the distance. He stood up and saw the back end of a black SUV racing and swerving down the street.

His cell rang. "Yes!"

"David, what's the matter? We have an appointment with Blander in an hour. Are you okay?"

"Sorry Marie but someone took a couple of shots at me. More damage to my car than to me, though."

"I'll send help."

"No need, I have a whole FBI to help me. I will meet you at the White House in an hour. The pictures I have will clear up part of the mystery."

Two FBI SUVs came screeching to a halt. Six agents flooded the area. David knew they must be getting close if they tried to kill an FBI agent. The meeting at the White House was now more important than ever.

Chapter Twenty-Two

President Blander was surrounded by security personnel who were giving reports on what, if anything, they heard on the 'chatter' listening posts. There was the usual posturing by terrorists but nothing specific. When Foster and Perkins walked in the President stood up. "Everyone, please leave the room."

David and Marie had their presentation all worked out. It had to be succinct and clear. There was much the President would not want to hear. "Agents, thank you for coming. What do you have for me?"

Marie began. "It now appears Alan Murphy is a sleeper agent. His real name is Ahmad Akbari and he has been in touch with a suspected ISIS cell in France. We also have photos of Murphy meeting with Vice-President Mason."

David followed up. "Bank records tie Murphy to Frank Bellows as well as Mason. We have exact amounts that Murphy gave Bellows being passed along to Mason. We don't know if Mason is a willing partner or has been seduced by the contributions and is unaware of Murphy's overseas connections."

The President looked at the evidence and shook his head. "All this is circumstantial at best. The meetings between Murphy and Mason may be just campaign contributions. Bellows left no journals or papers even hinting at Mason's role. And even your report says they think the man Murphy met in France is Behzad Hakimi."

Marie took out wire tap information. "We have phone logs and tapes of Bellows calling the house where his assistant, Greg Manners, was keeping you hostage. It was shortly after Bellows met with Mason that he told Greg to kill you."

The President took a second look at the evidence. "How do you suggest we proceed?"

David put out a plan. "Marie will target Mason. As deputy chief of the Secret Service she can infiltrate the Vice-President on the excuse of doubling the protection since you were kidnapped. I will go to France and investigate the meeting we were told about between Murphy and Behzad."

"Do you have a contact there?"

"Yes, I have worked with the Chief of Police, Jean Blanchet, in Wissembourg."

The President picked up the phone. "Arianna, call John Gold."

Marie handed the President an executive order form that would double the Secret Service guard around the Vice-President.

"Agent Foster. I will put NSA's Gold at your disposal. He will have assets on the ground in both Germany and France. Anything else you need?"

"No sir, thank you very much."

As David and Marie left the office Arianna walked in. "I'm sorry, Mr. President, I have some very bad news."

"What is it?"

"I have just been told that Victor March has died. I know he was very close to you."

David and Marie stopped, hopping they could offer their condolences. "We are sorry to hear about your friend's passing."

Blander spoke very quietly. "Victor March, retired army general, was my mentor when I was in the service. He selected me to be his driver all through France and Germany. He developed a love for France and moved there after he retired. He has been in a nursing hospital for about a year. He had inoperable pancreatic cancer."

Arianna held out a message. "I'm sorry, sir, but General March did not die of cancer. He was shot to death in the hospital by three gunman."

That news stunned everyone. The President banged his fists on the desk and David took the message from Arianna to check it out. "Why would anyone kill a man who was retired and dying?"

It was then that David saw something that created a new puzzle. "Mr. President, it says here that your friend was in Wissembourg, the same place Murphy met with Behzad."

Marie took the message and read it. "You don't think there is a connection?"

"Now I need to get to France as fast as I can. I do not believe in coincidences."

NSAs Gold made arrangements to have an agent meet Foster in France. The evidence might be circumstantial but it was all fitting together. Using a satellite phone in the White House David called Chief Blanchet. "Jean, this is David Foster. We spoke before about Ahmad Akbari and Behzad Hakimi. I am on my way to France and would like to meet with you."

"Of course, I will be glad to be of any assistance I can. You will have to excuse me right now as we just had a murder in one of the hospitals."

David's face lit up. "Was that the murder of Victor March?"

"How did you know that? What can you tell me?"

"March was a close friend of President Blander. We think there is a connection between the murder and the plot against Blander."

"I will have all the evidence by the time you arrive. The hospital is in the same area as Behzad's compound."

David hung up and told Marie what he had heard. "David, be careful. They will not hesitate to kill an American FBI agent."

"Don't worry, I can handle myself. Besides, we are getting closer and closer."

David was off to the airport and Marie headed for the Vice-President's office. Things were developing rapidly.

Chapter Twenty-Three

"Please come in. I will be with you in a minute."

Susan Star had conducted many interviews with powerful people but this was a first. She was about to sit down with the Vice-President of the United States.

"Thank you for agreeing to this interview. I will not take up much of your time."

Blander chose Alice Mason to be his running mate after his first choice had to 'retire' to 'spend more time with his family'. The truth was that during his college years he not only appeared in blackface but he was the lead debater defending the position of the founding fathers who allowed slavery to continue.

Alice smiled. "We have met before when I was a member of the House of Representatives."

Susan thought back. "Yes, it was during the debate on establishing full ties with Cuba. You were very persuasive."

"And I remember you as not one of those 'jumpers'."

"Jumpers?"

"Those press people who jump up and yell to get attention. They remind me of little children yelling 'pick me, pick me' in gym class."

Susan could not help smiling and chuckling. "That has never been my style as I have respect for the person and the office."

Mason sat opposite Susan. "I also have read just about every article you have written and they are intelligently done. You get right to the heart of the subject without the editorializing. You have an excellent reputation as a journalist and I hope your editor appreciates you."

"Unfortunately our editor is a CM and that is why I love to get out of the office."

Mason looked puzzled. "What's a CM?"

"Cave Man. His attitude and treatment of women would almost qualify as a hostile workplace. But that is for another time and I am on a deadline."

"Sorry, please ask away. And you can call me Alice while we are in my office."

"Thank you Madam Vice-President. Were you aware the President had been kidnapped over the Trade Bill?"

Mason smiled. "That is exactly what I am talking about. You continue to call me Madam Vice-

President as a sign of respect and your question gets right to the bottom line."

"I don't want to waste any of your time asking about your background which is well known."

Mason leaned forward. "The President was never kidnapped. He was involved in very delicate talks with several heads of state. That has already been reported on."

"Should you replace President Blander, would you follow his policies? It was rumored that you changed your position on the Trade Bill."

"I am my own person but of course there are many good things President Blander is doing that I would continue. As to the Trade Bill, I mentioned that I could stand behind it if new facts were presented."

"There is a story going around that your Press Secretary is about to resign. Any truth to that story?"

Mason stood up and walked behind her desk. She took out a group of folders and placed them on her desk. "Sally is leaving as she is pregnant and she wants to be an at-home mother. Off the record, she has had two miscarriages and she wants to do everything the doctor says to better the outcome."

"I am sorry to hear that. Of course I will not mention that."

"These files are interviews I have been conducting to replace her, although that will be nearly impossible. She started with me when I first ran for office through my time as governor and into the Vice-Presidency. I need a strong, intelligent woman who will represent me and be willing to work with the press."

Susan closed up her notebook. "I understand that. Those kind of people are very rare and hard to come by.

Mason stood in front of Susan. "I think you are one of those rare people who would represent me, and the country, at all times."

Susan looked puzzled. "Are you asking me to be your new Press Secretary?"

"Yes. I believe we would make a talented team and your job at the Washington World does not seem to be making you happy or provide you with advancement. You would work in the office next door."

Susan was dumfounded. "I never thought about something like that. I must admit it does intrigue me and I know I could handle the position."

Mason walked back to her desk and pushed a button. "We might as well get you started, just in case. The first thing is to be vetted by the Secret

Service so I have asked the head of my detail to come in."

Susan stood and faced the doorway as the Secret Service agent entered.

"Susan, meet my Secret Service team leader Marie Perkins."

The two women looked at each other with surprised looks. "Miss Star, it's nice to see you again."

"Yes, very nice."

Mason smiled. "Good, you know each other. Now we only have to get you vetted. Marie, who does the vetting?"

Marie started to laugh. "Vetting is done by the FBI, specifically by the Special Agent in Charge of the D. C. Office. His name is David Foster."

Chapter Twenty-Four

Foster's plane landed in Paris, from there he took the train to Strasbourg and finally a taxi to Wissembourg. He was met by Police Chief Blanchet and brought to a small room.

"How was your flight?"

Foster winced. "Long and I still can't straighten my legs. From what I have seen of France you have a beautiful country here. I can understand why the world comes to Paris."

"Yes, especially during the spring. Can I get you something to drink?"

"No thanks, I'm on a tight deadline and if what we think is going on is true, I can't afford to waste a minute."

Blanchet smiled. "You Americans are always go, go, go. You need to take the time to relax and enjoy the world around you."

"I agree. When this is over I will come back to Paris and just veg out."

"And will you bring your special lady with you?"

"Absolutely, if I can figure out who is my special lady."

They left the station and headed for the hospital where March was a patient, the Centre Hospitalier de Wissembourg. They met with March's doctor who confirmed that March was indeed dying of pancreatic cancer and would have died in the next three months or so. There were no clues as to who was responsible for the shooting. They showed pictures of Behzad to the other doctors and nurses.

"Yes, he is familiar. I was at the information desk and he asked for General March's room. I gave him directions and I think he was joined by two other men. It was not long afterward that I heard gunshots."

"Did you see him and his friends leave?"

"No. All I saw was the back room where I hid."

Blanchet and Foster went down to the hospital morgue to examine the body. There was nothing to see except for two bullet holes in March's chest. They talked with the coroner who gave them the autopsy folder. More proof that March would have been dead within three months.

"Thank you for your time."

The coroner shook his head. "I do not know why you came all the way to France to look at the body."

Foster handed back the report. "Why do you say that?"

"This man, General March, is scheduled to be flown back to Washington, D. C. for burial at your Arlington National Cemetery. I understand there will be a large gathering of dignitaries and your President will be there."

Foster was caught off guard as he was unaware of the funeral arrangements which included the President. If someone wanted to get the President out in the open this would be the way to do it. "Chief, I have to return to the U.S. right now. Can one of your men get me to Paris and the airport?"

Blanchet shrugged his shoulders. "Of course, but you just arrived. At least let me take you to lunch."

"I thank you but I have a feeling I must get back to the States. You have been very kind and when I return to Paris I will be more than happy to share a meal."

"Pierre will take you. I am looking forward to your return."

Foster climbed into the police car and headed for the airport. He took out his cell phone to fill Marie in. "Marie, I think I know what is going on. I am heading to the airport."

Marie was surprised to hear from him. "David, you just landed in Paris and now you are off again? This is not good for you physically. Why don't you stay at least until tomorrow."

"The body of General March is being flown back to the States. He will be buried in Arlington National Cemetery and the President will be there, out in the open. I think that is Murphy's plan."

"It makes sense. We will cover the cemetery like a blanket. I don't know how a shooter will get close enough to fire."

"Just get the layout of the cemetery and when I get back we will map out a plan. By the way, how did things go with the Vice-President?"

Marie chuckled. "I am now her team leader and she has asked me to help vet a new staff member. Her former press secretary is resigning and she has a candidate for the position."

"That was fast. I thought they took weeks to find just the right person."

"Mason found the right person while being interviewed. You will have to do a deep, very deep, dive into this person since we believe the Vice-President may be involved."

"No problem. Who is the person?"

Marie was just waiting for this moment. "Her name is Susan Star."

Foster looked like he had just heard the world was about to explode. He sat dumfounded and groaned loudly. The driver heard that sound. "Monsieur, are you okay? Do you need to stop?"

David snapped out of it. "No, no. Just get me to the airport as fast as you can."

Marie seemed to be enjoying the situation. She figured David was in shock and was not sure how to proceed. She could not wait until he was back on American soil.

Chapter Twenty-Five

The meeting room at FBI headquarters was filled to overflowing. There were agents from all Federal agencies. David arrived late and did not have a chance to talk with Marie although he was not sure what he would say. He looked at her face and there was a mischievous smile on her lips.

Marie began the meeting. "Ladies and Gentlemen, please take your seats. We have a lot to plan and not much time to plan it."

David rolled in a white board and set it up so the overhead projector image would shine on it. The lights were dimmed when suddenly the door opened. The Vice-President came in along with her new press secretary. "Please, continue."

Marie looked at David. Was this an example of the fox being in the hen house? They both had suspicions about Mason but no real proof. Here she would see all the precautions and all the security to protect the President. Not ideal, but there was nothing to do except continue.

David turned on the projector which displayed a Google map scene of Washington, D.C. He refined it to show the road from the White House to Arlington National Cemetery. "The President and the First Lady will leave the White House for the funeral of General March at ten o'clock. They will be in a special limo with bulletproof glass and steel reinforced doors. The good news is once inside the car, with six agents walking beside it, there is little to no chance of an attempt on them."

Marie handed out assignments to the agents along with security positions and codes. "The bad news is the cemetery itself. There is no way to seal it off and there will be so many individuals there that we cannot vet any or all of them. We will not know who is legitimate and who might be a terrorist."

One of the agents stood. "Marie, can't we funnel everyone at the entrance and have a metal detector check point?"

"Sorry, no. There will be other people who are not part of the funeral and that will create a huge backup."

"David, what about the bridge leading to the cemetery?"

"That bridge will be protected by coast guard boats, and helicopters will fly overhead to intercept any assassination plans. In addition, the Park Service will have their rangers on the bridge with a clear view of the surroundings. Again, as the President will be in the special limo, there is no major protection problem."

Vice-President Mason walked up to the board. "I noticed that this intersection could be blocked by a truck and terrorists could launch a handheld missile."

David put up another map. "As you can see we have already placed D.C. police to stop any vehicle from entering the intersection. In addition we have removed mailboxes and welded shut all sewer grates."

"Thank you."

Marie put up a diagram of the burial site. "There are many ways a gunman or gunmen could approach the site. The President and the First Lady will be seated in these chairs beside the grave. There are 360 degrees of open space beyond the site making it almost impossible to cover everything."

Mason spoke up. "Again, I am sorry to interrupt. Has any thought been given to surrounding the grave with bulletproof curtains?"

"That would block the view of the mourners and make it awkward for press coverage."

"You are going to allow the press to attend? That does not seem very wise."

"This is still an open democracy and the press is allowed to cover stories of public interest or concern. I am sure members of the press will be respectful and follow our instructions."

There was laughter from the room. "Again, thank you."

All the agents broke into groups to discuss each group's assignment and make recommendations for adjustments. The Vice-President left with her new press secretary close behind. There were still a million details to work out and some of them were conflicting. They only had two days to get it right.

David and Marie were by themselves. "So you think the general's murder was to force Blander out into the open in a place that is almost impossible to cover?"

"Yes, when I saw March had been shot close range and one of the nurses recognized Behzad I knew it was part of the attempt."

Marie pulled out a report. "This is the latest from the teams who are following Alan Murphy. He spent all of his time at his Solutions headquarters. There was a small gap in our coverage when a decoy car left the building. Murphy was not covered for about two hours. The only other thing that left the building were two trucks with symbols of paint cans and the slogan 'We Paint The World'."

David read the reports. "Solutions is supposed to provide private security. What were paint trucks doing there?"

"Perhaps they were painting the headquarters."

"I will visit Solutions and see what I can turn up. I'll pretend I am double checking on the group who kidnapped the President."

Marie nodded. "I don't think there is anything there but being safe is better than being sorry."

David put down the report. "When will you brief the President?"

"We meet with him at four o'clock."

There was a long period of silence between the two. David turned off the projector and erased the white board. Marie picked up any remaining printouts of security assignments. Finally David walked over to Marie, put his arms around her, and kissed her.

"What was that for?"

David spoke softly. "I missed you and I love you."

Marie could not let it go. "Did you see Mason's new press secretary, Miss Star?"

"I will take care of the vetting in a professional manner."

Marie smiled. "I wouldn't expect anything less."

She turned and left the room leaving David to deal with his uncertain future. Why was it so difficult for him to make a choice?

Chapter Twenty-Six

"Welcome to Solutions. How may I help you?"

David and another agent were signing in at the main desk. He was not sure whether Murphy would speak with him about the Germany trip but he wanted to try. Besides, this gave him a chance to look over the Solutions company. He noted the business had massive security with both a metal detector and a full body scan station. There were three armed guards in the lobby.

"Hello. We would like to speak with Mr. Murphy. We are from the FBI."

The receptionist looked up at David with a blank expression. "I'm sorry, sir, but Mr. Murphy only speaks with people who have an appointment. Would you like to make one now?"

David expected that. "Call Mr. Murphy and tell him we are here. I am sure he will see us."

"I am sorry but without an appointment there is nothing I can do. Perhaps you could speak to the unit manager."

David decided to push. "We are from the FBI and Mr. Murphy is a person of interest in a kidnapping and murder case. I can be back with a search warrant and go through the building looking for him if you would like."

The receptionist was shaking and hyperventilating. "Perhaps you would like to talk with our department manager?"

David nodded. "Yes. Thank you very much."

About five minutes later a man in a dark suit walked into the lobby. "Hello, I am Robert Zander, Vice-President of Solutions."

"Hello. I'm David Foster from the FBI and I wish to ask Mr. Murphy some questions."

Zander took a minute to look over the two men. "I'm sure Mr. Murphy would want his attorney present. Please check with him first and then you can make an appointment."

David took out a folded piece of paper. "This is a search warrant issued by a special court under the authority of the National Security Act. Since Mr.

Murphy is under suspicion of criminal acts which involve National Security we are allowed to search his place of business in order to find and question him."

It was a bluff. Zander did not seem the type of person who would block action by the FBI and certainly would not know anything about the National Security Act.

"Please, come this way."

David and his partner walked through the rotunda and stopped in front of the elevators. Two of the men from the lobby suddenly appeared along with two other men who came out of an elevator. "This looks a bit like obstruction of official FBI business. I hope you and your men are prepared to serve long sentences in a Federal Prison."

Zander smiled now that his men had arrived. "You must understand that what we do, and how we do it, is highly classified. Perhaps we could discuss this in the rear lounge. Please come this way."

David knew he was on thin ice. He turned to his partner. "Steve, handcuff him and his men. We'll call for backup and then take them all to the station."

It was now a game of who would blink first. Steve took out some zip ties and Zander and his men pulled guns but pointed them at the floor. They all just stood with no one talking or making any moves.

It was if they were playing that kid's game called 'Statue'.

Zander blinked first. "Put away your weapons. Mr. Murphy is not here and you can search if you want to. Frank will show you around."

David and his partner began an unofficial tour of the building. Murphy was not around but the two FBI men were able to gain a sense of the operation and how vast it was. They finally arrived in the main garage.

"I would like to see what's in that storage room."

Frank shook his head. "I am sure Mr. Murphy would not be in the storage room."

"He could be hiding knowing we are looking for him."

Frank folded his arms over his chest. "Sorry, but that is going too far. There is no reason to open that door."

David decided to try his bluff one more time. "Steve, handcuff Frank here and put him in the car."

"You can't do that. I have done nothing wrong."

As Steve took out his cuffs David again stretched the truth. "Under the special court's order, you are in violation of the National Security Act and as such I have the authority to place you under arrest."

Frank called to the garage foreman who came over with the keys. The closet turned out not to be a closet but led to another garage space where tools and paint cans were scattered about. The two agents inspected everything including the trash. Finally Steve came over holding an empty paint can. "David, there are wrappers indicating there were explosives in this garage. And based on the number of wrappers there was a large quantity here."

Frank immediately denied knowing about any explosives. "I have no idea what those are doing here."

David took out his cell and called headquarters. "Jacob, David here. Bring out the team and the bomb sniffing dogs. I have a feeling we are going to find additional bomb materials somewhere in this garage."

He next called Judge Paster. "Judge, David, I need an exigent circumstances warrant for Alan Murphy's Solutions building."

"Well, David, it's nice to hear from you even if it is only for a favor. What's the situation?"

"I am in Alan Murphy's business garage and we have reason to fear he has camouflaged some vans to plant explosives along President Blander's route to Arlington Memorial Cemetery."

"Reason to believe. Am I going to get bitten in the ass over this?"

"Would I let my favorite judge get into trouble?"

The judge laughed. "I'll send it over. Just don't do anything until it gets there."

Twenty minutes later four men, dressed in combat gear and heavily armed arrived in the garage. One of them approached David. "I'm Thresher. Mr. Zander says you have no warrant and he wants you to leave. NOW!"

"A warrant is on the way."

"But it isn't here yet and besides you have to wait until our attorney gets here and looks it over. NOW LEAVE!"

"Easy big fellow, no need to start anything. It's just that when we do leave a site the evidence always seems to disappear."

Thresher and his men drew pistols. "My men and I will escort you out one way or the other."

He moved closer to David and his men trained pistols on Steve. As if it were a Hollywood script, FBI agents arrived with the bomb sniffing dogs. The reinforcements drew their weapons and outnumbered Thresher and his men three to one.

With the situation under control, the dogs were let loose in the garage. It did not take them long to find something. David and Steve opened a carton and could smell the gunpowder and electronic fuses. There was no doubt that bombs would be placed along the President's route but exactly where was still a mystery.

As the FBI removed the material David called Marie. "We have another piece of the puzzle and I'm afraid it is not good news. Murphy stockpiled explosives and he is missing. We'd better work fast."

Chapter Twenty-Seven

"Miss Star? I am Special Agent Marcia Winters of the FBI. I am here to begin the vetting process. May I come in?"

Susan was not happy. She was expecting David to be doing the vetting. It would give her a nice opportunity to connect with him. "Yes, of course. Please come in."

"Thank you. The Vice-President requested this vetting for the position of press secretary on her staff. I will be asking questions that will be very personal and you are not obligated to answer them. There are no right or wrong answers. Once I have completed the interview I will check each and every answer you gave."

"Wow, I better be very careful. I don't want to lie to the FBI and wind up in jail."

Marcia smiled. "Do not worry about that. You are not part of any criminal investigation. Not telling the truth will hurt your chances of getting the security clearance you will need for the position of press secretary."

"Would you like something to drink?"

"No thank you. I will be recording this interview."

Susan started to breathe heavily, took in a deep breath, then tried to relax. "I thought Agent Foster did all the top-level vetting?"

"Yes, he normally does but he is involved in a delicate case and asked me to fill in. If you wish to wait for Agent Foster we can postpone the interview."

"No, no. Let's go ahead. Fire away."

"Just some preliminary questions. What is your height and weight?"

"That's a strange question, why do you need that?"

Marcia shut off the tape. "In case of an emergency, if we have to fly the Vice-President and her staff out, we need to know the combined weight."

"Five feet four and one hundred and nineteen pounds."

"I'm sorry, I didn't have a chance to turn on the tape. Would you repeat that?"

"Five feet four and one hundred and twenty-one pounds."

Marcia smiled at the increase in weight. "What is your age and occupation?"

"Twenty-six and I am a journalist at the Washington World newspaper."

"Do you have a criminal record? Have you ever been arrested?"

"Okay, this is getting tricky. Are you asking about recently or way back in the past."

Marcia shook her head. "Any time."

"I was arrested when I was fifteen when a group of us girls raided the boy's cabins at summer camp and threw all their clothes into the lake. Does that count?"

Marcia could not help but laugh. "Okay, tell me about the contacts you made while working in Washington."

"I have interviewed leaders and staff from Ireland, England, Nigeria, Poland, and China. I have been embedded with troops in Afghanistan. I am presently working on a story involving the Secret Service and the FBI."

Marcia looked up suddenly and seemed to be in shock. "Excuse me. You are investigating a case involving the Secret Service and the FBI?"

Susan continued as if she were telling a story. "And I am also dating Agent David Foster."

Marcia shut off the tape and put the machine in her briefcase. "I am terribly sorry but I cannot continue. I was not told about the investigation and your relationship with Agent Foster. My being here could be seen as obstructing the practice of the free press."

"You have not done anything to obstruct me. You are just doing your job asking questions."

Marcia closed her briefcase, stood up, and hurried to the door. "I will have Agent Foster get in touch with you. Thank you for your time. Goodbye."

Marcia was out the door and doing double steps to her car. She got in, gunned the engine, and sped away. Susan was laughing the whole time because she really did not care about the position, she just wanted to get Foster to her apartment.

Just as she shut the door her phone rang. "Hello?"

"Susan, this is David Foster. I just got a strange call from Agent Marcia Winters. Did you tell her you and I are dating?"

Susan was smiling. "I was supposed to tell the truth. What else was I going to say. We have been out dining and you have been to my apartment."

"Why did you do that? I will have to do a lot of explaining about our relationship. No, not relationship but ...I don't know what to call it."

"I am so sorry if I caused you any trouble. Why don't you stop by and we can discuss the exact nature of our relationship."

David felt he was in another one of her traps. He had strong feelings for Marie but Susan kept popping up in his thoughts. He would like to date her to see where it would go but that would end any chance he would have with Marie.

"Look, I am in the car heading back to the office. I have information that must get back to the President. Perhaps we could meet for breakfast and hash things out."

"It would be easier to have breakfast if you just stayed the night."

David was getting frustrated. "Susan, stop that."

"You mean you wouldn't want to spend the night with me? Am I that hideous?"

"No, of course not. I have to hang up now but I will see you tomorrow at seven at the diner."

"I'll be there."

Susan hung up and did a little spin dance. She was having breakfast with David, just the two of them. She picked up her phone. "Mary, come over. I have a story to tell you."

Chapter Twenty-Eight

"Mr. Murphy! Mr. Murphy! I have to talk to you."

Alan Murphy and his crew were just finishing up the renovation work in the control room of the Arlington Memorial Bridge. Along with paint and plaster, they were installing high explosives tied to a technological box that would respond to a signal from outside. The explosives were on both sides of the draw bridge location.

"I'm in the control room. What can I do for you?"

Park Ranger Nelson Parker arrived with his deputy and a file folder. "I'm sorry but you and your men will have to leave now. I just got word that the bridge is being put into a security one situation."

"That's no problem. We have just finished up both control areas and were about to leave. Is that okay?"

"Yes, of course. I have to do an inspection with my deputy before I seal the room."

Alan had to think fast. "Why don't I take you on a tour of the area so you can check things out and let me know if we did not do something right."

"That sounds okay. Let's start over in the panel station."

While Murphy and Parker were checking things out, his men were taking out paint cans that formerly held explosives. The deputy watched to make sure no souvenirs or bridge materials were taken. The paint cans were left open to show that they had held paint although the cans had been painted anyway to look like they had been used.

"Everything looks very nice. You and your men did a great job."

"Thank you, shall we exit?"

"Wait a minute. There is a pipe running along the ceiling being held up by column supports. I don't remember there being a pipe in that position, much less being held in place by column supports."

Parker walked over to the supports and started to pull on one. "This support is very rigid and appears to be able to hold much more than those pipes."

Murphy took out his cell phone. "Ranger Parker, I have a picture of the other side of the bridge where there is a control room annex. If you look carefully you can see the same pipe and support columns matching what is here."

Murphy was breathing rapidly. One of his men came up behind the ranger, took out a knife from his pocket, pushed a button and a four-inch blade suddenly appeared. He walked closer to the ranger.

Murphy caught the movement out of the corner of his eye. "Tres, why don't you take the step ladders out of the room."

Tres put the knife away and picked up the two step ladders. The ranger wrote something in his file, turned, and walked out of the room. Murphy followed him and quickly closed the door.

"Okay, I hope no one left anything inside because I am going to put this seal on the door. If anyone tries to open the door they will have to break the seal. My deputy will be in the main office watching the door on closed circuit. No one is getting in there."

Murphy extended his hand. "Thank you Ranger Parker for all your help. My men and I will file our bill and be on our way."

The trucks were loaded and the men started to drive over the bridge. Just as they did a black SUV passed them going in the opposite direction. The car came to a halt and David Foster and Marie Perkins got out. They walked over to Ranger Parker and introduced themselves.

"I'm Special Agent Foster of the FBI and this is Agent Marie Perkins of the Secret Service. We are doing a final check of the route the President will take on his way to Arlington National Cemetery. Has anything unusual happened here at the bridge? Anything at all?"

Parker thought a moment. "The only thing was a renovation company finishing up the repairs to the bridge control room. They were unable to finish before due to the Covid situation."

"Did you check out the company?"

"Absolutely. I also walked around the control room making sure everything was the way it was supposed to be. My deputy and I then sealed the room with a camera aimed at the door. We will know the instant someone tries to break in."

"What about the bridge deck itself?"

"I heard about the procession for tomorrow. I have called in all my men and we will go over the bridge one more time and then take up positions along the span. I have also called in bomb sniffing dogs to be sure there are no explosives hidden on the bridge."

"That's excellent. You should know that there will be coast guard and navy boats in the water blocking any water approach, and a helicopter will be overhead. My partner has a special code book for you to use in case of an emergency."

Marie took out the file folder. "Remember to call if you see anything out of order. We would rather chase down a mistake than overlook a real attack."

Parker took the code book. "Who is being buried?"

"General March, a very close friend of President Blander."

Parker nodded. "Yes, he has an excellent reputation. There will be a lot of traffic over the bridge."

Foster extended his hand. "Thank you Ranger Parker, I know we can count on you."

The two agents got back into the SUV and headed back to D.C. to meet with the President at four o'clock. Parker's assistant joined him. "They sure are nervous about tomorrow. I hope everything goes off like clockwork. By the way, here is the bill from that painting and renovation company."

"Great, I'll file it. Let me see, they are charging below the bid price and they did a super job. I just might hire them to do my house. What was the company?"

"Solutions Painting and Alan Murphy is the General Manager."

Chapter Twenty-Nine

It had been a busy day for Foster and Perkins. Right from the time the alarm went off until the final inspection of the Arlington Memorial Bridge, the pair crisscrossed D.C. meeting with all sorts of people. And it was not over yet, they were now in the Oval Office to update the President.

"Agents Foster and Perkins, thank you for coming. This is Harvey Black my chief of staff."

They all took seats on the couch. Foster began the briefing. "Mr. President, we have identified the source of the threat and the individuals who are part of the plot. We know that your friend, General March, was murdered in order to have his body flown back to the U.S. for burial in Arlington National Cemetery. Being a highly decorated war hero and your close friend, the goal was to get you out into the open where it would be close to impossible to control the area."

Perkins then took up the current situation. "Mr. President, we have taken steps to control everything from the time you leave the White House to the time you arrive at the gravesite. The entire route is protected by land, sea, and air components. The troublesome site is the cemetery. You will be in the open without any way of vetting the crowd or covering every hill and bush."

The President looked over the report. "So you believe the attempt will come at the gravesite. But if you know that won't the plotters know that? Perhaps they will try from some other vantage point."

"That is always possible but highly unlikely. We have been able to check and secure every street you will travel on. We also have imported a new limo with design changes that can stop an RPG and fifty caliber rounds. Even the rounds that penetrate body armor cannot penetrate the windows."

"Harvey how long is my speech at the gravesite. I would assume the agents would like a very short one."

"Yes, Mr. President. Normally you would pause to allow the crowd to applaud but since this is a funeral there will be no applause. The entire speech will run ten minutes."

"Well, agents, is ten minutes too long?"

Foster shook his head. "Even ten seconds would be too long. But we can work with this if Harvey can chop off part of it. I'm sure those attending the funeral would appreciate a very short speech."

Harvey nodded and left to rewrite the remarks. Marie took out a list of suggestions for the President. "Normally you stand and speak but we would like you to move around the grave, changing directions as you do. We have left a walking space for that. In addition if you were to kneel a couple of times it will give my men an excuse to surround you."

"You want me to play an old man unable to get up, is that it?"

"Yes, Mr. President."

Foster looked at Marie and then Blander. "We have done what we can. I hope it all goes well. We have hired actors who stand at least six feet four to surround the gravesite as well. It will be a sort of human picket fence."

The President stood up. "I cannot tell you how much I appreciate everything you are doing for me. I know it has been a long road but I feel very secure and comfortable in your hands. I will see you both tomorrow."

Marie looked at David and decided to bring up their doubts about the Vice-President. "Mr. President, there is some circumstantial evidence that Vice-President Mason may have had contact with some of the members of the group we believe is responsible for this attempt."

Blander showed no visual facial expression at the news. "Well, I am sure you will check that out. Thank you for that observation."

David and Marie shook the President's hand and left the office. As they did, Harvey was just coming in. "Four minutes, yes, four minutes."

Harvey went into the Oval Office while David and Marie walked down to the staff break room and poured themselves some coffee. They sat quietly as they both had been on their feet all day. Foster kept looking at his coffee and not drinking it. Marie looked at him. "David, what's wrong? We have a solid plan. You worry too much."

"It was something Blander said that bothers me."

"What was that?"

"He said if we know the only place the President will be vulnerable is at the gravesite, the plotters will know that as well. We may have missed something."

Marie leaned over and hugged David. "Take a deep breath and remember we have checked every inch of the route. It will take a tank to even put a dent in that limo."

"Well, it looks like our protection experts are taking a coffee break. I hope all the preparations are complete."

The two looked up and standing with a smile was Vice-President Mason. "I just heard there was a small delay in the vetting of my new press secretary. I wonder if you could explain what happened?"

Foster stood up. "Sorry, but I am not fully aware of the problem. We have been out all day getting the route ready for tomorrow's funeral procession. Will you be riding with the President and First Lady?"

Mason laughed. "Nice way to change the subject. But no, I will be stuck back here in case something does happen to the President. I know with your abilities everything will come off smoothly."

Marie took out her folder with the route plan. "Would you care to look at our plan?"

"No. I am sure it is very detailed as you have checked out every inch of the route. I would imagine the gravesite does create a problem."

David answered. "Yes but we have special plans for that as well."

An aide came out of the Oval Office. "Madam Vice-President, the President will see you now."

Mason looked at Foster. "Well, good luck. And get on that vetting process as I would like to have my press secretary in place ASAP. Things happen fast in Washington and I would not want to be caught unprepared."

As Mason walked away David and Marie looked at each other. "She doesn't look worried. Is she a part of it or not?"

Chapter Thirty

Susan followed the dirt road that took her deeper and deeper into the woods. It was getting dark and there would be no streetlights to guide her. She was following a lead from a subscriber who talked about a cabin in the woods where some very high-profile people lived. Since her vetting was delayed she figured why not keep busy.

She finally found the cabin but it was no rough-looking hunting cabin. While it had the rustic look, the grounds were well cared for and it was three times the size of a hunting lodge. She pulled up to the front and got out of her car. The first thing she heard was a motor of some kind. She walked around the side and saw two very large propane tanks attached to the lodge. A little further down she saw a home generator.

Back around the front she knocked on the door. There was no answer. She knocked again. "Hello? Anyone there? My name is Susan Star and I'm from the Washington World. Is anyone inside?"

Again no answer. She tried the door handle and the door slowly opened. She was faced with a beautifully appointed room that cost more than most apartments in the city. Directly in front of her was a floor to ceiling fireplace with wood stacked beside it. The mantel was covered with pictures. To the right there was a fully equipped kitchen with state of the art appliances. To the left was a dining area that could seat ten.

Suddenly a man appeared coming out of a side room. He was tall and looked rather menacing. "Who the hell are you and how did you get in here?"

"I'm sorry, the door was open and…"

"And you thought you would just walk in uninvited."

Susan began to back up to the door. "I really did not mean to disturb you. I will just be on my way."

She turned and opened the door. Standing in front of her was a woman carrying an overnight bag. The woman was familiar but the surprise of seeing her delayed the identification. Then suddenly her mind caught up."

"Madam Vice-President, how are you?"

Vice-President Mason had a deep frown and hurried into the room pushing Susan aside. "How the hell did you find this place? What are you doing here? Al, help me out."

The man, Al, grabbed Susan's arm and pulled her farther into the cabin. "Sit on the couch and don't move."

Susan looked down and saw Al was holding a pistol. She immediately sat on the couch. Mason stood in front of her. "Who else knows you're here? What do you want? I offered you a choice position in my new cabinet and you throw it all away by coming here. You would have been the first female press secretary for the first female president of the United States."

Susan was not sure she understood everything that was being said. How could she be the first female press secretary for the first female president?"

Mason turned to her friend. "Al, we have to do something. If she gets away she will print our whole story."

"Let me think a minute. If we kill her we have to hide the body but some fool hunter will find it after an animal digs her up."

Susan was in full panic. She suddenly stood up and pushed Mason who fell over. Just as she reached the door Al caught up to her. He spun her around and punched her in the face. She fell backward and lost consciousness.

When she awoke she was tied head to toe on a chair with tape over her mouth. She was able to move her head and turned it to the left. There she saw another man, tied up as she was, seated in a chair.

Mason turned Susan's head towards her. "You have really messed things up. But fortunately Al has come up with a plan. I'm just sorry it has to happen like this but we have no choice."

Susan struggled but she could not budge the ropes. Tears began to form as she faced the probability that she was about to die. Mason pulled the tape off her mouth.

"Since you are about to die I should introduce you to your roommate, my husband Jon Mason, soon to make me a widow. And this marvelous man with great hands and mind is Alan Murphy. Tomorrow morning President Blander will be assassinated while I arrive safely at the White House. By the end of the week I will be the President who took over after the untimely murder of President Blander. I will also be a grieving widow. That should help when it's time for my reelection."

Susan finally was able to talk. "Why are you doing this? You will never get away with it. The authorities have every inch of the funeral covered."

"Do you know how magic works?"

Susan was caught off guard with that question. "No."

"Misdirection. You see the police have looked at every possible way the president could be shot. They have even put him in a new limo that is bullet proof and bomb proof. But they missed the fact the president could die by drowning."

Susan shook her head. "That is not possible."

"My friend Al has taken care of that. His first idea was to kidnap the President and then have him killed but his plan was so complicated and involved so many people that it failed. This time the plan is perfect."

Al came back into the room. "Okay, I placed the device on the propane tanks and in about thirty minutes the tanks will blow and the cabin will burn to the ground. There is no one close enough to come to the rescue."

"Good. Load up the car. What did you do with her car?"

"I parked it up against the propane tanks."

Mason retaped Susan's mouth and smashed her cell phone so it could not be used to find her. Al left in his car and Mason left in hers. The lights were out and it was getting dark. All Susan could imagine was that David Foster would suddenly show up and rescue her.

Chapter Thirty-One

It was nine-thirty, and David and Marie were at the White House along with security personnel and the designers of the new presidential limo. Marie was making last minute checks with her agents while David was making his fourth call to Susan Star. Still no answer.

"David, has she picked up?"

"No, and that worries me since a good reporter never shuts off their phone. All I get is her mailbox. Something must be terribly wrong."

"Well, we have a much bigger worry, keeping the President alive knowing there is a plot to kill him."

David put away his phone but not his concern. He walked into a briefing room where the designer of the new limo was outlining his creation. Dr. Frederick Pinse had designed the limo around the same concept as used in safe rooms in homes. People were asking question after question as he showed pictures and diagrams of his design.

"Dr. Pinse, what if someone used a biological weapon that might be airborne?"

Dr. Pinse looked every bit a mad scientist that people came to expect of geniuses. "The doors on the passenger compartment are sealed tight. Once an attack is discovered the entire cabin is enclosed much like a space capsule. The doors have bolt locks and cannot be opened from the outside."

"Doctor, what about the windows? They cannot possibly withstand a high explosive placed on the glass."

"There are no windows in the rear compartment."

That statement drew a collective sigh and many side conversations, with the room becoming noisier and noisier. David tried to quiet the room but was having little success. "Doctor, I can clearly see the back seats. How is that possible if there are no windows?"

Pinse moved around to the front of the room. "What you are seeing is not through a window. The normal glass window has been replaced by the same technology used in computers and monitors. You are seeing virtual reality painted on the area where the glass would normally be. By doing that we can strengthen the door panels since we can eliminate the space needed to roll down the windows."

Marie waved her hand to be recognized. "Doctor, what you are saying is that the compartment where the President and First Lady sit will be totally encapsulated. How will someone open the door?"

"They cannot. Unless the inside occupants press an emergency release, the doors will not open."

Another agent stood up. "You say high explosives placed on the car will not cause damage and even firing a rocket at the car will have no impact."

"The outside shell material takes in the force of the explosion and harmlessly dissipates that force much like what you see in sci-fi movies."

The Attorney General walked up to Dr. Pinse. "Doctor, thank you for this explanation. We are about to leave and the President and First Lady are about to enter the new limo. Everyone to your stations!"

David and Marie got into an SUV and drove the route ahead of the motorcade. The funeral procession was led by two motorcycle policemen with an SUV of secret service agents behind. Next would be the limo and directly behind it was another SUV of secret service agents. Next would come high government officials followed by military commanders followed by members of the general public.

The trip was peaceful. There were many individuals standing on the sidewalk watching. Twenty press vans with dishes on top were stationed along the way broadcasting everything to the world. David and Marie sped forward to check out intersections and the bridge. Mailboxes had been removed and manhole covers had been welded shut.

The bridge was crowded with onlookers and security personnel lining the walkway. David pulled into a parking area at the end of the bridge. Marie waited in the car tracking everything in real time. David met with the Park Ranger commander.

"How is everything? The procession will be here in about five minutes. Anything out of the ordinary?"

The Ranger smiled. "Things are tight as a drum. I don't want the President to see me with paint all over my shoes and pants, so I'd better go change."

"What happened?"

"I was doing one final check of the control rooms under the bridge making sure the seals had not been broken. I wasn't looking where I was going and I stepped in a paint tray on the floor."

David laughed. "Let's hope that's the biggest problem we have."

"I hope so as well. The painters did a fantastic job and to leave the tray is not like them."

David was trying not to think about the cemetery problems. "Well, perhaps we can deduct the cost of your pants from their bill."

"Good idea. I am sure the people at Solutions Painting have enough profit to take…"

David suddenly interrupted and grabbed the Ranger. "What did you say!?"

"Just that Solutions Painting…"

"Who hired them? Who vetted them?"

The Ranger was getting nervous. "The foreman, Alan Murphy, had a signed order from the Vice-President's office."

David suddenly ran back to the car, pulled open the door, and yelled. **"Marie, he was here! This is where the attempt will be! Stop the procession!!"**

Marie was confused and had trouble understanding what David wanted. By the time it all made sense she looked at the bridge. The Presidential limo was on the bridge just about in the midpoint. David ran waving his arms trying to stop everyone. The motorcycle police spun around and the secret service agents who walked beside the limo pulled their weapons.

David was within fifty yards of the bridge when everything went dark.

Chapter Thirty-Two

Some witnesses say it was louder than a volcano eruption while others said it was more like a missile strike. People were thrown in all directions, and trees were uprooted and tossed like uncooked spaghetti. The fireball that was unleashed was tall enough and hot enough to melt two cell towers as well as cars on the ground. The scene resembled the aftermath of a tornado or a war zone.

When the smoke finally cleared, the middle part of the Arlington Memorial Bridge was gone. Missing. No longer there. The President's limo and the bridge roadway were first lifted into the air and then dropped into the Potomac River. Two Coast Guard boats were reduced to sticks and there was no sign of the crews. Civilian casualties would take days, or perhaps weeks, to count.

Marie slowly crawled out of the car. As she pulled herself up she touched the outside of the car door and burned her hand. When she stood up her vision was shaky at best but she knew she had to head toward the bridge. As she staggered along she came across David's body, lying in a twisted fashion with small fires burning his coat. She rolled him over putting out the flames.

Emergency vehicles began arriving in large numbers while people continued to run for their lives. Perhaps the most important question should have been who set off the explosion but it was not. The most important question was the location of the President's limo which was missing.

"David, David, can you hear me? Are you alright? Say something!"

David whispered. "Where…where…is the…President?"

Marie looked around at all the first responders running from body to body. "I don't know. I don't know. I can't see the limo."

Two EMTs knelt beside David and started to check him out. They put bandages on several burn spots and offered to take him to the hospital. "I'm fine. Leave me alone. Get to others who are really hurt. Have you seen the President's limo?"

"Sorry, no. Are you sure you don't want to go to the hospital?"

"Yes, now go help others!"

Two emergency field headquarter vans, which had been on standby, moved to the bridge perimeter and set up about twenty-five yards from the huge hole where the midsection of the bridge used to be.

"You are the highest-ranking survivor. What are your orders?"

David stretched as he stood up. Marie was by his side. "Get Dr. Pinse down here as fast as possible. Treat as many of the wounded as you can. Get me all the news footage of the procession. Begin a nationwide hunt for Alan Murphy and seize the Solutions business headquarters."

Marie got on the phone to her office. "Get to the Vice-President and put her under protective custody 24/7. If you see Alan Murphy take him into custody. Do not, I repeat, do not let the Vice-President leave the White House. If necessary tie her to a chair!"

"Agent Foster, I'm Captain Broadhurst of D.C. police. My men and I are at your disposal."

"Thank you, Captain. Get a Dr. Pinse from the White House and bring him here ASAP. Don't stop for anyone or anything. Have your men help with treating the wounded. Get a count as quick as you can."

The D.C. police left and the Coast Guard reported in. "We lost two boats and twelve crewmen. We have cordoned off the Potomac."

"Thank you. Help transport the wounded and check the IDs of everyone you come across. See if any of them speak French and asked them if they have been to France."

Marie moved beside David. "That French thing is not necessary."

"Well I think it is and just do it!"

"Dr. Pinse is here."

"Good. Send him over to the other van so we can talk in quiet."

David headed to the other van with Marie by his side. He had a splitting headache and the burns were giving him a lot of pain despite the pain meds the EMTs injected into him. He stopped and could not catch his breath so Marie slapped his face which energized him. "You do that after we are married…"

Marie smiled and put his arm over her shoulder as she helped him to the second van. "Dr. Pinse, where are you?"

"Look, we don't have a lot of time, so keep your answers brief."

Pinse had a diagram of the limo on a table. "From all accounts the limo is now sitting on the bottom of the Potomac. Due to the force of the explosion all emergency features were engaged. No water can get into the compartment although that is not true of those in the front seat."

"You say the President and First Lady are still alive?"

Pinse hesitated. "Yes, definitely but there is good news and bad news."

"Give me the good."

"There are extra oxygen supplies in the compartment so they will have air to breath. That gives us three hours to rescue them."

"And the bad news?"

"We cannot open the compartment until the limo is on dry land. Much like a safe room all the controls are on the inside but we cannot be sure the President is in any condition to use them. Once out of the water we can open the door."

David felt faint and backed into a chair. "Okay, Doc, I thought you couldn't open the door from the outside."

Pinse grinned. "I lied."

"Okay, what will it take to lift the limo out of the water?"

"You have to understand we never anticipated this kind of an event. The limo weighs as much as the M1 Abrams tank or about 67 tons."

David moved over to the radio operator. "Tom call the Air Force base."

"This is Lieutenant Stein. I heard about the situation. Do you know how the President and First Lady are?"

"Not yet. We need to get them out of the Potomac first."

Stein wasted no time. "How can I help?"

"I was told the M1Abrams tank weighs in about the same as the limo. Is there anything that might be able to lift the limo out of the water?"

There was a pause. "Yes, the MIL V-12 copter can do about twice that weight."

"How fast can you get one here?"

"Before you hang up the radio."

David leaned back and had trouble breathing again. Marie found the reserve emergency oxygen mask and put it on him. "David, you need to rest. I'll take care of the rest. Doctor Pinse, take care of him."

"But I'm not that kind of a doctor."

"You are now."

Marie left the van and headed to the coast guard boat tied up at the bridge. "Captain Sweeney, we need some special help."

Sweeney came off the boat. "What do you need?"

"A helicopter is coming to lift the limo off the bottom. We need divers to wrap the compartment with steel cables to attach to the copter."

Sweeney thought a moment. "Divers we have, but that much steel cable we don't."

Marie thought a moment. "I'll call my brother, he's a construction supervisor, and I'll tell him we need cable like yesterday."

"Okay, I'll send trucks to pick it up. Do you think the President is still alive?"

"Yes, and we intend to keep him that way."

Marie ran back to the van and found David lying on the floor. Dr. Pinse was adjusting the oxygen mask and trying CPR. Marie went to the emergency medial kit and took out the heart paddles. She sat beside David. "Don't you dare die on me. I will never forgive you if you die!"

Chapter Thirty-Three

Beep! Beep! Beep! Beep!

David turned his head and opened one eye. The beeping woke him and he wanted to hit the snooze button for just a little more sleep. But there was no night table with an alarm clock, only a monitor box on a tall metal pole. As his eyes began to focus he could see a white board with his name and other items written on it. He tried to roll on his side but it caused a sharp pain in his arm and when he looked he saw he had an intravenous tube.

He lay back and realized he was in a hospital and the beeping came from some kind of machine. He moved his head to the other side and saw a nurse coming in. He tried to speak but nothing came. The nurse pushed a button on the machine and the beeping stopped.

"Oh, you are awake. I will get the doctor."

It seemed to take forever until the doctor arrived. "Agent Foster, I am Dr. Lopez and I am treating you for your injuries. Can you speak at all?"

David used all his energy. His voice was raspy and soft. "What am I doing here? Is the President okay? I must get back to the bridge."

"Sorry agent but you are going nowhere. I have detailed orders to keep you here even if I have to tie you down."

"Who gave that order? I'm a Special Agent of the FBI."

"At this point you could be the President and I could not let you go. My orders, and threat, come directly from a Marie Perkins of the Secret Service."

David relaxed. "Okay, okay, what is wrong with me?"

Lopez took out a chart from the end of the bed. "Besides being way too close to a massive explosion you have suffered heat burns to your lungs and throat and you have a concussion. I heard you ran the rescue operation and calmed a lot of people before you collapsed."

Now David was agitated and tried to get up. "What is happening? What time is it? Where are my clothes?"

"You are not leaving, so get that idea out of your head. It is twelve-thirty."

David lay back down. "Has the President been rescued yet?"

"They are still working on it. If you promise to be a good patient I will turn on the television and you can watch what is happening."

Lopez turned and switched on the television. All channels had the same live coverage of the attempt to rescue the President. "To finish, you have scorched lungs and you are weak because you cannot get enough oxygen. You also have a mild concussion which is the cause of your dizziness. While your last tests show improvement, it will take perhaps weeks for complete recovery. I will be back later with your new test results."

The doctor left the room and David focused on the television. He remembered that the President's compartment had enough air for three hours and it had been two and a half by now. The nurse brought in ice water and Jell-O but he wanted neither. He kept watching and praying.

"This is Brandon Sharp at the Arlington Memorial Bridge covering the rescue attempt of President Blander and his wife. The effort so far has involved cables coming from a construction site, Coast Guard divers in the water, and the biggest helicopter I have ever seen. There is a press briefing about to start."

David watched as press people surrounded the speaker. It was Marie; she looked tired and disheveled. "I will make several statements to catch you up. I ask that you take into consideration my exhaustion."

Behind Marie was Dr. Pinse, two men dressed in Coast Guard uniforms, and three uniformed police officers. "At about ten fifteen this morning the President's limo was about to cross the Arlington Memorial Bridge on its way to Arlington National Cemetery. An explosive device destroyed the center span of the bridge causing the President's limo to fall into the water and drop to the bottom. Rescue operations are ongoing and we plan on placing steel cables under the limo and then a helicopter will lift it. Colonel Bright of the Coast Guard will explain the operation."

Bright came forward. "We are going to wrap steel cables around the compartment housing the President and First Lady. We were fortunate the limo landed upright on the portion of the bridge that also sank. This gave us room to thread the cable under the compartment. A MIL V-12 helicopter is circling the area."

A reporter waved his arm and shouted out a question. "Colonel, how can you be sure the President and First Lady have not been killed by the explosion or have drowned."

Pinse stepped forward. "My name is Dr. Pinse and I designed the limo prototype. The compartment is totally sealed so no water can get in. There is emergency oxygen that will keep them alive. The compartment is built like a home safety room and is double secured. When the helicopter lifts the limo we will be able to get them out. Lifting such a weight out of the water causes multiple problems including the suction of the water itself."

Another reporter shouted out his question. "Is there any word on casualties?"

The D.C. police chief stepped forward. "Presently, the unofficial total is eighty-five confirmed dead and two hundred and thirty injured and taken to hospitals. The dead and injured are from security personnel, first responders, and members of the crowd. In addition several SUVs caught fire and many inside were killed."

Then came the most difficult question. "Do we know who is responsible for this attack? Are they terrorists from overseas or home-grown?"

Marie came forward. "That is all the information we have and can release at this time. We will keep you updated as the investigation continues."

David's medication finally kicked in. He could not keep his eyes open and he drifted off to sleep. He continued to pray as long as he could.

The doctor came back and saw Foster asleep. He turned to his nurse. "Let him sleep and call me the minute he wakes up. He will be happy with his test results but he has a long recovery ahead of him."

The nurse turned off the television and straightened out Foster's blanket. Events at other locations were still happening but for him the day was over.

Chapter Thirty-Four

Marie Perkins found herself in command of an unprecedented operation. She had to balance the Air Force helicopter, the Coast Guard divers, the arrival of construction equipment, and security around the entire area. Fortunately since she was being pulled in so many directions she did not have time to worry or panic.

Her command center was a command post van with enough computer power and communication gear to run a small city. With a staff of six from different agencies it was amazing how well they worked together.

"Agent Perkins, I have the Chief of Police on the line."

"This is Marie."

"A very strange thing has happened. We found Alan Murphy, in of all places, in the White House office of the Vice-President."

"Chief, you have to trust me on this. Place men around that office and don't let Murphy or the Vice-President leave. I will send some of my people to reinforce your men."

"You want me to arrest the Vice-President!"

"Believe me it is something that must be done. We have evidence that she is connected to the plot."

The chief hesitated. "I'm not sure I can do that."

"Please. I will take full responsibility for your actions."

"Okay but I am not happy about it."

Just then her brother, the construction manager, entered. "Sis, sorry, I mean Agent Perkins, the cables are being wrapped around the compartment. Underwater welders are attaching the hook to the helicopter's lines. We have two separate cables in case one breaks. The strain on those cables will be tremendous."

Marie rushed out of the van to view the scene for herself. There was a massive crowd all around the site and just as massive a security presence. Ambulances and fire-fighting equipment surrounded the hole in the bridge and Dr. Pinse was standing by to offer directions on how to open the compartment from the outside.

"This is Brian Elliot reporting from KLAC news. The helicopter is beginning to rise and the cable attached to the limo is taut. I can hear the strain of the copter's engines as it tries to pull the limo up. There are other cranes on either side of the gaping hole that have also been attached to the cables."

Marie watched knowing there was nothing more that she can do or could have done. She looked at her watch and it was almost three hours since the limo sank. Slowly, very slowly, the helicopter began to rise. The cable squealed and the wound strands that make up the cable suddenly snapped. Despite the size of the crowd there was complete silence except for the helicopter.

The helicopter stopped rising and descended a bit. The divers went back into the water to weld more of the cable to the side of the limo. Another line from the helicopter was dropped and wrapped around the connection area of the cables. With a thumbs up from the divers the helicopter started to rise again. The water began to churn and waves became visible. Then the top of the limo was out of the water.

Marie had been holding her breath. She resumed command. "Looks like they have it. Get Pinse out here so he can direct the rescue team on how to open the compartment."

Marie walked over to Pinse. She had to shout as the helicopter noise made it almost impossible to be heard. "How do we get the door open? Should we cut into it with a torch? Do we need explosives?"

Pinse leaned close to Marie's ear. "There is an emergency system that will blow the doors off hopefully without hurting the President or the First Lady."

The sudden cheering from the crowd drowned out the noise of the helicopter. It was an amazing sight, something you tell your grandchildren about. The limo was out of the water and resting on the shore. Emergency personnel, ambulances, construction crews, security, and Pinse surrounded the vehicle. Marie could only stand and watch.

Pinse was in command. "You two, cut the cable three feet from the bottom of the compartment. You, get oxygen ready, they will need that immediately. You, get me a hammer and a chisel. You, get those stretchers ready."

With hammer and chisel Pinse opened what looked like a small door. He next pressed buttons in sequence and there was a small explosion. The construction workers pulled the door open but did not know what they would find. The television cameras tried their best to focus on the occupants. There was almost total silence.

A lone figure stepped out of the limo. "Thank you for coming for us. We were a bit concerned."

It was President Blander who had crawled out of the limo and then stood to address the crowd. The

First Lady was still seated. "So what has been happening since that very loud noise?"

"Mr. President, please sit down and put on this oxygen mask. We have to transport you to Walter Reed along with the First Lady."

Marie stood and watched. She had done it; she had saved the President. She had not stopped since early in the morning but her day was not done. Individuals came up to her for orders. Top level government leaders and heads of various military branches all turned to her for coordination. The crowd was cheering loudly again and yelling 'Blander, Blander, Blander'.

The television anchor was at a loss for words. "I cannot tell you the relief and happiness that has spread through the crowd. From my vantage point the President and First Lady do not seem to be injured. Now the investigation begins as to who was behind the attempt. For that part of the story we go to Jack Backman."

It was over. One President saved; one assassination attempt thwarted. Marie felt like crying but her mind suddenly flashed to the face of David Foster. She had no idea how he was or where he was. She had to find him. She needed to be with him. She loved him.

Chapter Thirty-Five

Marie made sure the situation was handled and then headed for her car. But before she could get in a police officer stopped her. "Agent Perkins, we just got a call from the Vice-President. It seems she is demanding to meet with you."

Her day was not over and David would have to wait. Arriving at the White House she was met by her top assistant Falkner. "Welcome back. It must have been quite a scene at the bridge. Are you okay?"

Marie grunted. "We have to face the Vice-President and her friend. I need to explain some things to you so you will understand what I have to do."

Falkner nodded his head and when he had heard the full story his mouth dropped to the ground. He had trouble believing such a plot was in place but he had full trust and confidence in Marie. They both went to the Vice-President's office.

Outside the office the Chief of Police met her. "Nice to see you Agent Perkins. As per your orders the room has been sealed and we have cut off all communications. I'm not sure they even know about the bridge explosion."

"Thank you, Chief."

Marie and Falkner entered the office and were greeted by Vice-President Mason. "What the **hell** is going on? I am a prisoner in my own office! I need to talk with the President ASAP."

"I'm sorry Madam Vice-President, I am afraid everything was done under my orders. Who is this gentleman?"

"That is Alan Murphy, my new chief of staff. Whatever you need to say you may do so with him in the room."

Marie put on her saddest look. "I am sorry to inform you that there was an assassination attempt on the President's life. He did not survive. The President and First Lady are dead."

There was no expression on Murphy's face and Mason did not seem surprised. "What happened?"

"Someone planted a bomb, actually two bombs, on the Arlington Memorial Bridge and detonated them just as the President's limo was going over."

"I thought the limo was some special prototype that could not be penetrated?"

Marie put on her best sad face. "Yes, that's true, but it was never tested in water. The limo landed on its side on the bottom of the Potomac. We could not raise the vehicle or drill holes to supply oxygen."

Mason walked over to her desk and picked up the phone. "The line is still dead. I need more information and I need to take charge. I feel like LBJ on the plane back from Texas. I need to be sworn in."

Falkner walked over to Murphy. "It seems Mr. Murphy is not who he claims to be. We had word from a Chief Jean Blanchet in France that Mr. Murphy is really Ahmad Akbari and is part of an ISIS cell."

Murphy suddenly backed up into the corner. "That's outrageous!! I am a decorated soldier and proud American. Who is this Blanchet that you rely on?"

Falkner took out handcuffs. "He captured a man named Behzad Hakimi and destroyed the ISIS cell. Your name and picture were on materials seized by the police."

"That's impossible. You are making that up. Please, Madam Vice-President, do not believe them!"

Mason was caught in a bind. If she defended Murphy and they really had the evidence, she would be compromised. If she did not defend him then he might confess and drag her down with him. "I think we need to wait until the evidence arrives before we take any action. I will keep a close eye on Murphy so he will be available for questioning."

Marie took out a folder from her briefcase. "It seems you have already been keeping a close eye on Mr. Murphy. We have telephone records between you and Mr. Murphy."

"Of course, he is my new chief of staff."

"True, but some of the calls went to France, the same area where Mr. Murphy travelled to and met with Behzad. As a matter of record, there is even a call to you from Behzad when Murphy was not in France."

"The record must be in error. Someone is framing me!"

Falkner shook his head. "It also seems you transferred fifty thousand dollars to Behzad four days ago."

Mason was trapped. "Murphy threatened me and that money was for blackmail. I am a strong supporter of Blander and would never want to kill him."

Marie put the final nail in her coffin. "Here are records of you and Mr. Murphy staying at a motel in Maryland when you went to visit Dr. Pinse.

He told me that you spent a long time going over the limo prototype asking questions about any weaknesses. He remembers you were accompanied by Mr. Murphy when he told you about the water issue."

"I want to speak to my lawyer. Everything you say is a lie. I loved the President and supported him in every way possible."

Suddenly a voice came from the doorway. "That's very interesting. The head of the party told me about your plans to run against me."

Mason looked over at the doorway and saw President Blander. "But you are dead. I heard the explosions. I want my lawyer."

Four officers came in with the President and arrested both the Vice-President and Murphy. One of the officers handed Marie a message from Jean Blanchet. "Agent Perkins, we have investigated Behzad's cell. There is no record of your Mr. Murphy ever meeting with Behzad. And also, there is confirmation that Ahmad Akbari was killed three years ago in a drone strike. I do not know who your Mr. Murphy is. Good luck."

Marie called after Murphy. "Who the hell are you?"

Murphy looked back. "I want my lawyer."

Marie ran like a runaway train until she entered David's hospital room. She ran past the doctor, nurse, visitors, and her boss as if they were not standing there. She wrapped her arms around him and stared into his eyes. But she kissed his lips so softly it was like a touch of a butterfly.

David lifted her in an embrace. "Well, I am glad to see you. How have you been?"

They laughed as the last thirty-six hours had been absolute hell. Marie wiggled. "Put me down already!"

"Only if you promise to stay put."

It was then they noticed all the people in the small room. "Okay, doctors stay, and everyone else out."

Dr. Lopez picked up David's chart. "I have good news and better news."

"Go for it."

"The latest tests show your lungs are healing and you should be able to go home in a couple of days. That's the good news."

Marie put her arm on David's shoulder. "What's the better news?"

"David can return to active duty, but I kind of left the impression with his boss that he needed at least a week to recover."

They shook hands and the doctor left. A stranger walked into the room and looked very uneasy and very upset. "Agent Foster, I'm afraid I have some devastating news for you. My name is Ralph Young and I am the Assistant Editor of the Washington World. I was Susan Star's direct boss."

Young's words hit both David and Marie like a blow to the head. "What are you trying to say?"

Young cleared his throat and was having trouble speaking. "Yesterday morning forest rangers helped put out a fire in a cabin in the deep woods. The place was leveled and parts of two bodies were found. Outside there was a vehicle that was also destroyed, the only thing left was a license plate."

"For heaven's sake get to the point!"

"The plate traced back to Susan's car. During the police investigation they found enough DNA to match one of the bodies to Susan."

David sat back on the bed. "Who was the other body?"

"We cannot be sure but it appears to be Jon Mason, husband of the Vice-President. The arson squad said there was a device planted on the propane tanks that caused them to explode."

Marie put her arm around David. "I'm sorry, sweetheart, I know you cared very deeply about her."

Tears came to David's eyes and Marie was crying quietly. "Mr. Young, thank you for bringing me the news rather than my seeing it on television. I promise when I am back at work we will find the person or persons responsible for their murders."

Next to come in was Falkner, Marie's assistant. "Charges have been placed against Vice-President Mason and Alan Murphy. Unfortunately we still have not been able to identify Murphy. We have no idea what his real name is and who he was working for."

"I thought he was working for Mason?"

"No, she was unaware that he was tied to an ISIS cell. As it turns out Murphy is not working for the cell but using them much like he used everyone else."

David disappeared into the bathroom and when he emerged he was dressed in street clothes with his shield and gun on his hip. Marie reached out to grab him. "Where do you think you're going? Get back into bed, now!"

David looked at her. "I will either go around you or through you. Move!"

Marie followed him down to the parking lot where he got into the driver's seat of her car. She quickly opened the passenger side door and got in just as he peeled out. "Where the hell are you going?"

"I intend to get the truth out of Murphy, one way or another."

"David, please, you're scaring me."

"Let's hope I can do the same to Murphy. His lawyer has submitted papers, so Murphy will be released later today."

David's driving was as erratic and fast as an angry man could drive. He pulled into the parking lot of the Secret Service headquarters building and left the car so quickly that it had not come to a full stop. Marie had to grab the key to shut the engine and stop the car.

Once inside David the lobby he came up to the security gate. The guard came forward. "May I have your name and the purpose for your being here?"

David took out his badge and continued walking. "Hey, come back here. I need to search you. I'll have you arrested!"

Marie came to the gate. "George, it's okay, he is with me."

She caught up with David at the elevator and they rode up to the second floor holding cells where detainees wait before they are released. Sitting on a bench was Murphy, arms folded across his chest, eyes closed as if he were napping. "Guard, I'm David Foster, Special Agent in Charge for the Washington, D. C. FBI office. I have a warrant for Alan Murphy and I will take him to FBI headquarters."

The guard approached Foster. "I'll need to see the warrant."

Foster grabbed the guard. "Do you know who Murphy is?"

The guard pulled free. "Yes, he's the bastard who almost killed the President and First Lady."

"He also killed a woman very dear to me as well as the husband of the Vice-President. He is about to be set free and then we will never see him again. Is that something you can live with?"

The guard stood motionless and stared at David. He then walked over to the cell. "Murphy, your ride is here."

Marie tried to intervene. "David, not like this. Please!"

David grabbed Murphy and put on cuffs, perhaps a little too tight. He pushed Murphy toward the door causing him to bang into the wall. Murphy then 'accidentally' tripped going downstairs and then fell when he got to the car. Marie went with them hoping David would cool down before he did something that would force her to confront him.

Chapter Thirty-Seven

They arrived at FBI headquarters and Murphy was placed in an Interrogation Room. He was handcuffed to a table, and to be sure he wasn't beaten or killed Marie stayed in the room with him. The door opened and David came in carrying a folder.

David sat opposite of Murphy. "Thank you for agreeing to come to FBI headquarters and being willing to answer some questions."

Both Murphy and Marie were stunned by David's demeanor. He was calm, showed no signs of anger and was proceeding according to rules. Murphy laughed. "You beat me, pushed me up against walls, and tripped me on the stairs. That does not seem like proper treatment. And I never volunteered to come here and answer any of your asinine questions!"

David leaned back. "You feel I have mistreated you?"

Murphy laughed. "That is an understatement!"

"In that case I believe you are entitled to launch a formal complaint against me. I have a form here you can fill out and we will act on it."

Murphy was confused but not as much as Marie. Murphy's handcuffs were removed and he was given a form and a pen. He filled it out, signed it, and handed it back to David. Marie wanted to say something but did not know what to say.

David got up from his chair, opened the door, and a man entered. He wore the badge of the FBI and his name tag read 'Assistant Director Roger Matter'. He approached Murphy. "Are you saying you wish to proceed with this complaint against Special Agent in Charge David Foster?"

Murphy nodded. "Yes, Definitely. I hope you take his badge."

Matter left the room and was passed by Murphy's lawyer as he entered. "I see the games are finally over. Now release my client and we will leave."

David sat down. "I'm afraid we cannot do that. "Mr. Murphy is under arrest for perjury and obstruction of justice."

Marie shook her head but all she could do was watch. The lawyer laughed. "Still playing games are we? I will get a court order to not only release my client but also to bar you from ever approaching my client."

David continued. "Alan Murphy is not really Alan Murphy and we have proof of that. Just who he is we still do not know. But he signed this complaint form under penalty of perjury which he committed when he signed 'Alan Murphy'."

The lawyer first looked confused and then his face began to get red. "What kind of double talk is that?"

"If you wish to still represent your client I suggest you take a seat and keep quiet."

Murphy started to yell. "It doesn't matter if I am Alan Murphy or not! I am here and I can use any name I wish."

"Not true. If you use a false name in commission of a crime that is in itself a crime. Now if we had your real name and identity you could add that to the complaint and there would not be any perjury."

The lawyer looked at the form. "Okay, we withdraw the complaint."

"I'm afraid you cannot do that. The complaint is already with the investigating officer and has to be followed up."

The lawyer leaned over to whisper in Murphy's ear. "Just give them your name and we will be out of here. We will sue these idiots and collect a bundle of money."

Murphy backed away. "No way. I am not giving them what they really want. I'm not stupid, you know."

Suddenly Marie moved forward. "I just remembered that Mr. Murphy was the foreman of Solutions Painting and he submitted a bill for his work. He signed that under penalty of perjury as all government documents demand. It looks like my department will also be pursuing charges."

Murphy was in a bind. The penalty for perjury was up to seven years in jail and now he faced two counts. He thought about his real employer and what would happen to him in prison. He began to sweat and was breathing faster and faster. "You know what they will do to me? You cannot protect me in prison. They have ways of doing things."

David slid the copy of the complaint form back into his folder. "Have you ever heard of our witness protection program?"

Murphy seemed more nervous than before. "Yes. I will make a deal."

The lawyer stood up. "That's enough. We are leaving and we are not falling for this nonsense."

David walked over to the door and signaled to the agent standing in the hall. "Please escort the attorney, and if he refuses to go, arrest him."

Marie was now sitting at the table. "This is your one chance to save your life."

Murphy pulled out a handkerchief to mop his brow. "My real name is Andrei Sidorov of the SVR."

David smiled. "Russian Foreign Intelligence Service."

Murphy continued. "I was assigned this job as I have been deep undercover in the United States for over twenty years. My family must go with me."

"Why the assassination plot?"

"I convinced Vice-President Mason we could get rid of the President and she would be installed. We have been having a long-term affair and I would become her chief of staff. Being in that position I could pass along all sorts of information to Mother Russia."

Marie was writing as fast as she could. "Who developed the plans, made the contacts with ISIS, and supplied the materials?"

"It all came from the SVR directory under the orders of …Putin."

Putin's name struck chords in both David and Marie. Here was the first factual evidence connecting Putin with espionage in America. Murphy went on. "We came up with this plan because our interference in your elections did not pay off."

David pressed. "Are you saying that Putin and the SVR have interfered with our elections?"

"I will say no more until I have a signed agreement for the witness protection program."

David shook his head. "Oh, I'm sorry. I did not offer you a place in the program, I only wanted to know if you have ever heard of it. As a mass murderer and deep-planted spy you will spend time in prison, whatever happens."

Murphy jumped up. "NO! NO! You cannot do that! You promised. I will not last a day in prison and my family will be killed. You cannot do this!"

David and Marie left the room and stopped just outside. They could still hear Murphy yelling and protesting about what had happened. Marie was torn between the savagery of the deal and the need to get justice for all those killed at the bridge, at the hunting lodge, and other places they had not yet heard about.

David took out his cell. "David Foster for President Blander."

"Agent Foster, I just heard about the confession and the great work you and Agent Perkins have done."

"I'm sorry. Did you just say you heard about the confession that we just got minutes ago?"

"News travels fast in Washington. Why not come by tomorrow morning and we will sort everything out. In the meantime I will release a statement that we have caught the terrorist who bombed the bridge."

The President hung up and David worried about the politics of the situation. Would Blander publicly release all the facts or would he seal the records? Whatever happened he and Marie had done their jobs.

Chapter Thirty-Eight

Epilogue

June, three months after the assassination attempt, David and Marie were finally taking the step they should have taken years ago.

David shook Blander's hand. "Mr. President, it is an honor to have you here at our wedding."

"You and Marie make such a beautiful couple. It is too bad the rest of the world will never know what you did in the name of justice. Because of your work we have obtained the release of four Americans being held in Russia and we were able to identify the 'Russian Bear Hackers' who have been creating havoc with our internet services."

Marie walked up dressed in an off-the-shoulder gown. "It is nice to see you outside the office, Mr. President."

Blander smiled. "You are still one of the best agents ever on my protection detail and a very beautiful bride."

"What is next for you, Mr. President?"

"Re-election is just around the corner and I won't have to worry about Russian interference. And thanks for suggesting Senator Sloan for Vice-

President. I'm afraid Alice Mason will not be eligible to run or vote."

David took a deep breath. "We were sorry to hear about Andrei Sidorov, or Alan Murphy, but it is what it is."

The President nodded. "At least his American family is in the Witness Protection Program and all are safe."

Marie leaned forward and kissed the President on the cheek. "Don't worry, I will not do that in public while on your protection detail."

"Where are you two off to?"

"Honeymooning in Iceland to see the Northern Lights. Then back home for my new position as Assistant Director of the FBI."

There was a loudspeaker announcement. "Will the bride and groom come to the main floor to cut the wedding cake?"

The happy couple watched as the President and First Lady left. Having the President officiate at the wedding was something they would never forget. And watching the President try to dance will bring smiles to their faces for years to come.